CARTLAND INSTITUTE
FOR ROMANCE RESEARCH

The Colditz Cock

An **ULTIMATE HOLDING COMPANY** Publication

THE COLDITZ COCK
CARTLAND INSTITUTE FOR ROMANCE RESEARCH
An Ultimate Holding Company publication

First published in Great Britain

First Edition

Copyright © 2012 Ultimate Holding Company

ISBN: 978-0-9572628-0-5

Conditions of sale
This book is sold subject to the condition that it shall not, by way of trade *or otherwise*, be lent, re-sold, hired out or otherwise *circulated* without the publisher's prior consent in any form of binding or cover other than that in which it is published *and without a similar condition including this condition being imposed on the subsequent purchaser.*

This book is set in Baskerville

Published by:
Ultimate Holding Company
Hotspur House, 2 Gloucester Street
Manchester, Lancashire, M1 5QR

Commissioned by Tatton Park Biennial

Made and printed in Great Britain
by Calverts, London

The Colditz Cock

Author's Note

This novel is inspired by, rather than an exact account of historical events and characters.

The Colditz Cock is the name of a glider constructed by World War Two prisoners at the infamous Colditz Castle. Allied forces liberated the prisoners before they had a chance to put their escape plan into action. However, two replicas have been made of the glider and both have proven airworthy.

The female heroine of the story is based on a young Barbara Cartland. In addition to her prolific career as a writer, Cartland was also instrumental in the development of the air towed glider, which was used to transport troops during World War Two.

Coincidentally, the glider division of the British Army was based at Tatton Park at this time.

The invasion plan referred to by the British War Cabinet is based on Operation Market Garden, an unsuccessful Allied military operation fought in the Netherlands and Germany. It was the largest airborne operation up to that time and according to some historians flawed, by poor logistical planning, over confidence, failed radio communications and sun spot activity.

Some actual names and titles have been re-used by the authors, but the characters themselves are not intended to accurately represent specific individuals.

CHAPTER ONE

"Leave my supper on the night stand" Mary sighed to her housemaid.

Gisela dutifully set the silver salver down in the corner of the room, carefully moving aside a small amethyst brooch and the collection of treasured photographs.

Mary sat gazing out of the window, through the mist that had settled on the lake. "Shall I draw back the curtains a little and set a small fire for you in the grate?" Gisela suggested.

"No thank you," replied Mary, "I shall retire early. I will eat in a little while and then go to straight to bed." Then she added with a sigh, "I'm feeling unusually melancholy today."

Mary knew that, with no appetite to speak of, the food would stay untouched all evening, just as she knew that Gisela would surely make good use of the plate of cheese and ham to satisfy her own hunger.

Perhaps she should make more of an effort to eat? After all, she was the lucky one. Her thoughts wandered towards home, to her brother and sister far away in London.

She couldn't imagine that they would have feasted in such luxury for many months. Despite her family's standing and position, rationing meant good food was scarce, even for them.

Gisela moved to speak once more to her mistress, but sensing the mood, she turned around and quietly withdrew from the room, leaving Mary alone.

Mary looked small, almost childlike. Perhaps it was the

grandeur of the room in which she sat that made her seem so tiny.

She felt so small and lost in the world since it had descended again into conflict.

World events had engulfed her and divided her family. It seemed to her that all hope of happiness was a distant dream.

In private, Mary's face had begun to betray a growing desperation.

In London before the War she had been the belle of the ball, the debutante with whom everyone had clamoured to dance. Naturally warm hearted and radiant, the beautiful dark brown pools of her eyes gave her an exotic air which could capture the heart of any admiring suitor, and she had known how to use them to her advantage.

Her pretty rosebud lips were highly kissable, and kissed she had.

Mary's pretty oval face was framed by a stylishly set demi-wave; the height of fashion and the perfect frame for her eyes.

Many men took the sparkle in those eyes to be that of a woman in love, and she had a tendency to fall in love all too easily. But Mary's eyes were also a window into her very being, revealing a fierce intellect and questioning mind that could compete with any man.

Sat alone now in the window, her eyes rested on a small framed photograph of her mother which she had lovingly placed on her night stand. The sudden memories of home, and of the warmth and comfort of her mother that she longed for so much, brought tears to Mary's sad, brown eyes and little droplets of sorrow began to fall across her pale face.

"How has my life come to this?" thought Mary, as she sat, forehead pressed against the cold glass of the window. She was trapped in a foreign land, with a man that she felt perhaps she no longer loved, and there was not a thing she could do about it.

Even her family were powerless to help, not that her pride would have allowed her to entertain any kind of 'rescue', even if it were remotely possible.

Mary let out a sigh at the thought of her bad luck.

Had her mother, whose opinion she so respected, not warned her against marrying "that German"? Hadn't her brother urged her not to leave England for the Continent? Well, it was her bed as the saying went, and she would have to lie in it.

Her tears were interrupted by the brusque opening of the door and the appearance of her husband.

Heinrich Strauss, or to give him his full title Baron Heinrich Von Strauss, was a tall, imposing man with an air of danger about him. Mary regained her posture with a little start, as she suddenly remembered how attractive this had once seemed to her young, impressionable heart.

When he walked into a room, everything in that room came to a hault. Mary had stopped in her tracks when she first saw Heinrich.

His piercing eyes, his strong chin and aquiline nose, and his confident gait had caused her to catch her breath.

He commanded absolute attention and respect from those around him, and Mary was no exception.

Mesmerised by his presence at the ball one evening and then by the athletic power he had shown during an afternoon's riding, she had fallen into his arms in an instant.

With little thought for the future, she had left her home and her family to follow Heinrich to Germany as his wife. How foolish she felt now. How she regretted ever catching his piercing stare.

His stare was upon her now as Heinrich crossed the room and his firm hands pulled her to him.

Today in the cold light of the castle, those eyes did not instantly provoke feelings of love; instead she felt a little crushed, like a small bird in his powerful arms.

Turning her face away from his so as to conceal her private tears, she spoke quietly. "I was just preparing to eat and then retire. I feel weary and a little unwell. Perhaps I caught a chill on my ride out yesterday."

Mary spoke uneasily.

"You should take more care" said Heinrich, as he kissed her tenderly on the neck, pulling her small body even closer towards his, "my little English Rose, you must take care not get caught by some over-zealous patrolling soldier."

"You know you are safe here and the Commandant will tolerate you as long as I fund his 'little parties', his cigars and his brandy, but he would be powerless to stop a passing SS unit from rounding you up for a slice of their own glory."

Sternly Heinrich concluded, "it is not safe for you my love, in these dangerous times of desperate men."

At these words, Mary began to tremble.

She wasn't sure if it was her fear of the dreaded SS or resistance to her husband's rough grasp that made her body shake so.

"Of course, my darling, I am always careful to avoid causing you any trouble," she said.

"I stay within these grounds and speak to no one outside, as you know." Mary paused for a moment then spoke again.

"I would never endanger you, your position, or our life here."

A weak smile spread across her lips as she dutifully reciprocated her husband's kiss, but her mind was now elsewhere and she longed be alone with her thoughts once more.

"I shall leave you to rest my darling, but please, think more carefully about your little adventures into the wild outdoors." As Heinrich said this, his hand momentarily gripped

Mary's wrist a little too tightly, "I would not want any harm to come to you. It is for your sake that I say this."

It was true that Heinrich's strong and manly deportment still inspired admiration and some passion in Mary, but she was slowly beginning to wonder if her life in the castle was that of a prisoner and that perhaps her luck would be better if she had stumbled into the arms of a stranger in the woods.

Mary composed herself and withdrew from his grip. She then turned from her husband and took up her place at the window seat looking across the gardens.

Heinrich bade her farewell and left for what was undoubtedly another long evening of brandy and stories with his Party friends at the nearby prisoner of war camp.

. . . .

It was the following afternoon and the sun had broken through the earlier mist, bathing the gardens in a warm, golden glow.

From her vantage point at the window, Mary could see a beautiful expanse of endless sky framed by the dense green borders of the grounds below.

The well kept lawn, like an untouched oasis a million miles from the conflict that raged around it, continued to produce tiny summer flowers right up to the castle's formal borders, full of roses of every hue.

Sweeping down to the walls below, the expanse of green and pink was interrupted by three statuesque beech trees, to the side of which lay a small lake.

Today, the brilliant blue reflection from the summer sky had given the murky water a glass-like sheen and Mary was certain she would be able to see her face reflected as clearly as in a mirror.

As she sat letting the thoughts and colours of the afternoon wash over her, Mary noticed an unusual dark shadow pass across the lake's surface.

"A bird of prey, perhaps an eagle," she thought, "let me get my spy glass".

As she rose, she realised that this was no large bird sailing across the sky.

Looking up, Mary began to make out the mushroom-like form of a billowing parachute.

Transfixed, she watched as closer and closer it came until she was able to see the figure of a man falling, his descent slowed by reams of silk.

"His fall is quite graceful", she found herself thinking, "almost beautiful against the bruising late afternoon sky". The parachute's slow descent mesmerised her. For an instant she forgot her own sorrow as her whole being focussed on the scene in front of her.

Finally, after what seemed like an age, the falling man reached the ground, lurching to one side on impact as if hurt.

Involuntarily, Mary jumped to her feet, clutching ever tighter at the telescope and pressing it to her eye.

"That, if I am not mistaken, is an English RAF uniform." She could barely move her hands as she struggled to focus the glass.

"A British pilot. He must have been forced to bale out."

Now she could see a funnel of smoke creeping into the sky from the other side of the valley. "His plane must have crash landed over there. Now it won't be long before they come looking for him."

Until now and quite remarkably, it seemed that no one else had spotted the pilot.

None of the house staff were running into the garden and there were no soldiers on the scene, although Mary concluded that they would not be far away.

Mary stood and once again that day tried to compose herself. Her mind raced, wracked with confusion by this sudden event.

She took in a deep breath and closed her eyes, trying to focus her mind on the choice in front of her.

"Should I go to him? He is after all my countryman," she thought aloud.

"But what of my husband? It wouldn't just be my own life that would be in mortal danger, if I were to be discovered helping an enemy of the people."

The thoughts and fears came thick and fast; "what would become of me if I were caught by the SS? Heinrich certainly would not be able to protect me."

She wondered desperately what to do. Her life in England and her excellent but sheltered upbringing had certainly not prepared her for this.

Standing now, with her back to the scene outside, Mary knew that the time had come to make a decision. A decision that would echo across the rest of her life. Who should she betray? Her husband or her country?

She stood motionless, barely breathing for what seemed to be an age. Opening her eyes, resolve spread across her face. Her shoulders rose as if she had found her inner strength for the first time. She knew what she must do.

. . . .

The sun seemed to be toying with Mary as it slowly followed its downward course towards dusk.

She paced along the length or her room between the window and the bed. Mary maintained her usual routine, requesting a small plate of cold meats, pickles and salad which she took in the sitting room.

Just as every night, she read poetry for a short while in the well stocked library, this evening choosing a volume of William Wordsworth; it looked to Mary as if it had hardly ever been read.

Heinrich was not partial to poetry and the book was no doubt only in the collection to bolster his reputation as a man of letters.

She opened a page by chance and her eyes glanced at the words before her: A Wren's Nest.

> *Among the dwellings framed by birds*
> *In field or forest with nice care,*
> *Is none that with the little Wren's*
> *In snugness may compare.*
>
> *No door the tenement requires,*
> *And seldom needs a laboured roof;*
> *Yet is it to the fiercest sun*
> *Impervious, and storm-proof.*

She thought of her own nest, the cold castle and the English soldier by the lake.

"If only I could find a way to protect myself against the storm of events," she uttered aloud as she rose from her chair.

"It is not yet 7pm madam" exclaimed Gisela, who had been attending nearby "will you be retiring early this evening?"

"Yes, I fear I still have a chill and I will read in my chambers. When Heinrich returns, please explain to him that I have retired early and that I would prefer not to be disturbed?"

"As you wish madam" replied Gisela, "I will make up the guest room in the East Wing in case it is needed."

"Thank you Gisela, once you are finished you may retire early yourself. I am sure my husband will have no further need of you this evening."

With this, Mary turned her head away, a sign that the conversation was now over and that Gisela should leave the room.

After waiting for what seemed like hours, but was in fact a few minutes, Mary left the drawing room and emerged into the corridor.

Rather than turning left towards her room, she quietly made her way towards the kitchen. Without making a sound, Mary pushed gently against the kitchen door, nudging it open so that a slim shaft of light shone onto the table in front of her.

Darkness! This meant that the staff had retired and that she was alone in the house.

The servants' quarters were adjacent to the house in an old stable block that had been converted by her husband for this purpose.

He had always favoured discretion and privacy at his home and once the war had started this had become an imperative.

Heinrich's relationship with the ruling Nazis was secured by his vast wealth and social standing. The Nazis needed funds and Heinrich needed protection for himself and his English wife.

An unspoken understanding had grown between him and local officials; as long as his money continued to fund the war effort and the lifestyle of its generals, he would be left alone to live as he chose.

Only two members of staff were allowed in the vast house, Gisela the maid and her mother Gerta who acted as cook. Such arrangements were commonplace in the houses of German aristocrats, as in those of the English.

Gerta's mother and grandmother had served Heinrich's family and the ties of loyalty were strong. They had, over time, grown fond of Mary despite her provenance.

In fact, they saw Mary as the softer, more creative influence that Heinrich and his imposing house desperately needed.

They had watched curiously at the way this unusually practical English girl had involved herself about the castle, choosing the satin drapes that had been made for the sitting room and the delicate, flowered wallpaper.

Mary's knowledge of home-making had of course been drilled into her by her mother, but Mary's other more practical skills, and her love of poetry, had been sought out alone, quite privately and this was not a normal thing; for a girl of such standing to be so educated in words and science was frowned upon in society.

Gisela and Gerta were safely ensconced in their quarters as Mary began her secret work in the kitchen with newly discovered determination.

In the larder she found smoked cheese and Bratwurst, a large loaf of crusty bread by their side.

She gathered them up in a muslin found discarded on the kitchen table, carefully tying them into a bundle.

From a shelf she picked up a bottle of beer, two apples and she carefully filled a flask with water drawn from the pump.

Now, under the cover of darkness, she stole out of the kitchen door into the German night.

CHAPTER TWO

The carriage lurched forward awkwardly, jostling its tired passengers.

A sudden change in rhythm from the two horses harnessed to the Stanhope, had rudely interrupted Nell's slumber and she blinked wearily as she awoke.

All the elation and excitement of travelling in a horse drawn carriage had drained from the attractive face of Parliamentary Private Secretary Fenella Layton.

No one ever referred to her by her full name or title of course, she was simply 'Nell' to all her friends and colleagues.

The Prime Minister, her employer, had scarcely called her anything else since her first day in the job, which was twelve years ago almost to the day.

This familiarity was attractive to Nell and she often felt that it was one of the few relaxed features of her otherwise highly pressured and impersonal work.

"I'm getting too old for this nonsense!" she thought, "When will these ridiculous budget cuts stop?"

It had been less than a year since the Prime Minister's introduction of the Carriages Act, but it already felt to Ms Layton to be a very tiresome joke indeed. What was perhaps more galling was that despite the obvious necessity of the legislation, it was proving a very unpopular policy in some key constituencies.

As a mere private secretary, Nell knew her opinions were not to be called upon, although on occasion the Prime Minister and other Members of both Houses would stop her in the corridors of power and draw upon her vast canon of knowledge and experience.

She was never so improper as to overstep the mark, at least not often. "One day," she thought "my private impressions and opinions will make a best-selling memoir." After a sigh to herself she finally spoke aloud. It was the first time she had spoken in some hours.

"Surely we must be approaching the house? It is almost dark and we've been travelling all day."

"I'm afraid I'm not entirely sure where we are," came her travelling companion's coughed reply, through a pungent cloud of pipe smoke.

"A typical answer", thought Nell. He's never entirely sure about anything these days.

The journey north had been arduous and taken many hours and for the majority of the time Nell had avoided looking at her companion at all, choosing instead to watch the passing scenery or to doze.

She looked at the Prime Minister now and felt as if it was the first time she had really examined his face properly in years.

Prime Minister Major John Charleston was a decorated war hero who had served in the Great War. He was of good aristocratic stock; his father, the Duke, had first introduced him to Nell at a country ball many years previously.

Back then, Nell reminisced to herself, she had been the object of many a man's affections. There had even been a brief rumour of a liaison between the pair, but this was little more than idle gossip. Their past closeness was a distant country which she chose never to revisit.

By all accounts, Charleston was a bland man, although not entirely unattractive. Despite having relatively good sight, he wore huge, thick rimmed spectacles. He also seemed to suck permanently on a large brown pipe and both of these traits only served to obscure his few promising facial features: a strong jaw and elegant nose.

Nell recalled that in his youth the Prime Minister, or 'The Major' as the press referred to him, was once quite dashing and roguish, except for what had always been a greyish pallor to his skin and something akin to an ingrowing mustache.

Nell herself had lost none of her beauty and charm. Very fair, with piercing misty blue eyes, Fenella Layton had been blessed with a privileged upbringing and had been the toast of St. James's from the moment she appeared on the social scene.

Her husband, like so many brave souls, had been taken by the Great War and Nell remained a widow.

Even though she had been married and rather comfortably off, Nell had chosen the path of a career girl, politics was her passion and now her life. Her family did not understand her choices. Why would a young woman waste her looks and charm on the dark corridors of Whitehall? And so, her career had ostracised her from her father and mother.

Nell's day dream was interrupted as the horses' hooves left the metaled surface of the road and turned an abrupt corner.

Now there was only the crunching sound of gravel to replace the constant 'clip-clopping' that had accompanied them since London.

To Nell's sudden delight the landscape seemed to open up before them. She sat upright on her cushion and drank in the scene.

The carriage was passing through grand parklands. Majestic trees formed ranks at each side of the road which snaked gently now amongst acres of luscious rhododendron bushes, exploding in every shade of pink.

"How charming and utterly, utterly romantic!" she gasped.

The Major looked blankly back at her for a second, then

returned to reading his papers.

The glory of Tatton Park, the War Cabinet's new home, was wasted on him after such an arduous journey.

. . . .

Tatton Park was under an intense military lock-down on The Major's orders and everywhere, soldiers and staff hurried about their urgent business.

The people of Britain were completely unaware that Lord Egerton had graciously lent the entire house and grounds towards the war effort. The whole estate had been rapidly and almost completely transformed.

Parachute troops and soldiers were massing from every part of the land, undertaking secret training and practice jumps before being dropped into enemy territory.

Tatton Park now not only held a secret airstrip, but was also to play host to the entire War Cabinet.

Nell and the Major watched with interest the gathering military activity as they approached the mansion from the long driveway.

Of course, the recent land invasion of Europe had been a success, but now the Government and military were stealing themselves for counter offensives.

The British Generals and now the Americans were desperate for answers to the next big question; what now to defeat their common enemy?

The carriage slowed to a halt at the grand Romanesque entrance to the mansion and stationed itself next to several other horse drawn vehicles.

All around them were batteries of anti-aircraft guns. Every window of the grand house was criss–crossed with tape and protected by banks of sandbags.

To the wide eyes of Nell, the impressive scene was made

somewhat comical by the occasional hindrances of a passing herd of antlered fallow deer.

Stood between the entrance pillars and several aides and soldiers, Nell noticed the Prime Minister's wife Charlie; a stunning brunette, elegant and as always dressed in the latest fashions.

Before the war she had appeared in the daily newspapers almost more than her husband.

She was several years the Major's junior and this had caused quite a stir in certain circles.

Charlie was a Booth by birth and not of aristocratic stock. She had made her own wealth fighting to the top of her profession as a successful barrister in the Old Bailey. It was a world dominated by men in which her light shone brightly.

Few in the Prime Minister's circle trusted her and Nell was often saddened by this colouring of the woman's character. She had always found Charlie to be very good company on long nights working at Number 10.

Nell suspected that Charlie's detractors were envious of her success, or male chauvinists who ought to move with the times. The war, she believed had the potential to change everything.

Now they were dismounting the carriage and making their way to the door.

Charlie smiled at Nell and rushed down the step to greet her with a kiss on each cheek.

"So glad you made it in one piece!" she cheered. "Welcome to our new home in the country!"

She then kissed her husband twice and smiled weakly at him. "Let's get you all settled in."

The Major had not looked up from his papers during their arrival, noted Nell. Charlie, ever the alert and accommodating lady that she was, had not challenged him. She merely checked herself without faltering and fussed over Nell instead. The party entered the mansion between soldiers who presented their arms as they passed inside.

If the outside was busy, thought Nell, the inside was like Piccadilly Circus.

The blur of familiar and unfamiliar faces was dizzying to her after so long a journey.

Charlie held her arm and talked non-stop about the beautiful mansion. "Even though I have stayed in so many country houses, and under much happier circumstances," she exclaimed, "this has to be the most wonderful estate I have ever seen." The Prime Minister's wife seemed relaxed and gushed with excitement; "the beds, Nell! My goodness you will sleep like a baby!"

Charlie Charleston was, Nell had noted, already dressed for dinner. On the steps she had shone like a beacon in her full–length figure hugging yellow gown.

Nell could see how it shimmered now in the electric lights of the large hallway. Everyone else looked drab in army uniforms and suits.

Charlie still held Nell's arm as she gently but quickly guided them threw the noisy throng.

She cut through the men as they argued, pointed at maps and waved papers at each other. She seemed to glide across the marble floor like a ship.

"How have you been coping with this awful clamour?" remarked Nell, trying hard to be heard over the noise. "This is worse than Prime Minister's questions!"

The Prime Minister himself had abandoned the pair to their own devices, swallowed by a crowd of jostling Generals and Cabinet aides.

As Charlie dragged Nell out of the hall, past the Music Room and down a packed corridor, she managed a glance back over her shoulder.

She thought she could make out the red faces of the

Right Honourable Nigel Stalker and his insufferable wife, stood next to the influential and highly respected owner of a London department store. Yes, she was sure it was them.

Nell recognised his fawning smile from many a private dinner the Prime Minister had hosted at Number 10.

Nell felt repulsed as she realised that even at this dreadful moment in her country's history, these men were positioning themselves to make money.

Then almost completely hidden in the crowd she saw the only man she really wanted to see.

Trapped in animated conversation with a member of his staff was the ageing but upright figure of Major Maurice Egerton, 4th Baron of Egerton and Lord of the whole Tatton Park estate.

Maurice was so handsome, thought Nell and she noticed again that he had lost none of his charm and good looks. Maurice, or Lordy as he had always been known to her family, was dressed in a sharp and exquisitely tailored navy blue woollen suit, expensive but understated, perfect for a man of his influence and position.

Nell could see that in his hands he held a device that looked like part of a field radio transceiver, complete with wires hanging from the back.

Lordy looked up from his conversation and paused in his gesturing to the device. He smiled warmly as he noticed Nell and waved, then checked himself suddenly as he realised the radio was slipping from his other hand. Back into his heated discussion he was immediately drawn. "I'll talk to him later, when I've settled in a bit," thought Nell.

Charlie deposited Nell in her room and left her to get accustomed to her elegant surroundings in her own time. Dinner would not be for another hour or so, she had been informed.

Across the room, next to the ornate vanity table adorned

THE COLDITZ COCK

with golden cherubs and a fresh bouquet of pink roses, Nell could see that someone had already delivered her luggage.

One bag lay on its side on the light green coloured carpet. Another, to her surprise and embarrassment lay already opened at the foot of her bed.

Some fastidious serving maid had, presumably during an attempt to locate and carefully hang her blouses and skirts, been into her most private belongings and laid them out for her in neat order.

There, on the crisp linens for all to see, was an almost transparent pink lace negligee.

"Oh good heavens!" she exclaimed to herself. "This will never do! What if someone saw it?" she panicked to herself, hurriedly concealing the item beneath a more modest article from the suitcase.

Her secret weapon safely concealed, she let out a sigh of relief and slumped on the bed. Hopefully, only the maid had seen this embarrassing piece of nightwear.

Nell was however, quite aware of the loose tongues of serving maids and staff in large houses. She stood up and crossed the room, checking the bag on the floor. Yes, she could assure herself that the other bag had remained unopened and that the make–up and alluring perfumes it contained had not been discovered. This was a relief. If this weekend was to go as she planned and romance and love to be restored, the Prime Minister's private secretary would have to be more careful.

CHAPTER THREE

The moon was almost full in the clear night sky and shining its silver light in shafts across the lawns.

"Just like the search lights at the prison" thought Mary. She shivered at the idea of that cruel place. The thought of what went on in there at once terrified her and spurred her on in her mission.

With a clear view across the front of the castle and down to the valley beyond, she scanned the scenery, looking for where she had earlier spied the fallen airman.

The beech trees were casting heavy shadows towards the now dark water of the pond. Shadows shifted eerily in the gloom.

"Was that a figure?"

She ran quickly and quietly across the lawns, moving from shadow to shadow as fast as her shoes and dress skirts would allow, until she reached the water's edge.

The reeds had obviously been disturbed; imprints of heavy boots marked the soft ground.

"Where could he be? Where would he have hidden himself?"

"Oh my, what if I'm too late? Could he have been captured!" Mary felt the onset of panic.

"Maybe I should have told Heinrich after all," she thought to herself, "perhaps he would have been sympathetic to the man's plight and potential injury?

Then she calmed herself. Heinrich would never have helped. She scanned the facade of the home that had become her prison, with her husband as her jailor and thought again.

"Where would be the perfect place to hide?" she spoke into the night. Looking anxiously around, it came to her and she exclaimed aloud; "the barn!" Picking up her bundle of food she made her way amongst the shadows to the corner of the adjacent field and the overgrown barnyard.

The old barn was the perfect hiding place. Ramshackle, unused and dirty, it was obviously rarely visited by the grounds keepers and the safest hideaway on the estate.

The large wooden doors were twisted by age and no longer provided any security for livestock, had there been any, or the farm machinery stored inside.

In fact the doors were twisted far enough away from the frame that there was probably just enough room for an adult to squeeze through them.

Approaching cautiously, Mary glanced around to check that she was not being observed and then pressed through the gap, dragging her bundle behind her.

Once inside, it took a few moments for her eyes to become accustomed to the gloom. She could make out the silhouettes of discarded farm machinery, an old ladder, part of a car engine and broken gardening tools. The smell of hay and old engine oil filled her nostrils.

The vaulted roof had not been watertight for many years and fine shards of moonlight pierced through the dark wood creating pools of light on the rough floor.

It was in one of these patches of light that Mary found her first clue. In the half darkness were a few torn strands, the remnants of parachute cord.

Slowly and fearfully, Mary edged forwards, clutching at her bundle for protection. Her breaths came fast and although she tried with all her might she could not quieten herself. All the time she tried to listen carefully for any movement around her.

From somewhere in the murkiness there was a sudden clattering sound, as if a pail had been knocked over. It made Mary jump with fright, but instead of turning to flee, she leaned bravely into the dark, in the direction of the noise.

"Don't be afraid, I am here to help you," she addressed the darkness.

"I saw you land in the grounds. I know you are injured. I don't have much t..."

A gloved hand shot out from behind her and clasped across her lips, cutting short her words and stifling her gasp of surprise.

Mary felt another arm grab her around the shoulders and secure her arms tight across her body. She realised instantly that to struggle was futile and that even now her fate was sealed.

The man behind her was either a desperate wounded English airman, or a vicious SS patrolman and certain disaster. Mary, helpless against events, didn't resist.

Slowly, the hand across her mouth loosened its grips, and Mary was able to speak.

"I'm not afraid. Reveal yourself to me!" she panted in English. Then, composing herself, she repeated her words in German adding "don't you know who I am, let me go!"

There was no response.

Sensing that by now if her assailant really was a German soldier, she would have either been released or received a shouted demand for proof of her identity, Mary began to breath more slowly.

"I'm... I'm not afraid, but I know you must be." Then without pausing or caution she tried to blurt out the whole tale.

Mary felt the hold on her shoulders soften. Slowly the stranger in the dark turned her around and, as he did so, was revealed in a shaft of moonlight, a dashing English soldier. Mary felt an uncontrollable quiver race through her body.

His eyes met hers and he said, in a far kinder tone than she was expecting, "so we've established that you are not afraid, my dear girl! But perhaps you could tell me what exactly you are doing out here?"

"I saw your parachute land in the gardens, by the lake this afternoon...you were wounded...as you fell. I thought you..." she stumbled over the words, it was so long since she'd spoken anything but German.

"I'm a friend. I'm here to help you," she continued. "You are safe here for now, at least I think so." She looked at him and searched his shadowed face for a sign that he understood.

"Nobody else saw you land. Please...you must trust me." She paused again, a little perturbed by her obvious failure to communicate.

After what seemed like an age he suddenly smiled and in his smile she melted, embarrassed and blushing.

"I know. What I meant to ask was what on earth is a beautiful young English girl doing on a German country estate in the middle of a war?"

She looked up at him, her eyes filled with tears, her lips trembling despite her best attempts to hide it.

He thought that he had never seen anyone quite so lovely. "I suggest you start by telling me your name."

Dropping her eyes to release them from his piercing gaze, she answered: "I'm Mary. Mary Strauss."

"Strauss?" he repeated. "You married a German, and you are still here. You are either playing a very dangerous game or are very much in love!" he laughed.

And with that he regained his grip on her, taking a shoulder in each of his strong hands. "So, which is it? Which side are you on? Why did you come to find me?"

Fear darted across his face, "well I suppose I'll find out soon enough, if Jerry comes bursting through the door!"

She cut him a glance from her tear-filled eyes "I would never betray my country, however roughly it treated me."

The remark was deliberately pointed and as she made it she attempted to shrug off his tight grip.

"I take my vows to country and to my husband seriously. When the war first began, I truly thought it would be over in an instant and that the best place for me to be was by Heinrich's side." Mary had repeated the story in her mind so many times, in the hope it would become the truth.

"I thought we would soon be back to normal and that my presence here would protect him in some way. How wrong I was," she began to sob.

"It is I that needs protecting. I am trapped here. My husband offers me my only protection, and if I anger him, that could disappear in an instant."

There was no mistaking the fear in her voice, or the colour that had disappeared from her face. She raised her eyes to his and he thought she looked very young and very frightened.

"Then we are both trapped in a hostile place and both afraid." His voice softened, it was the kind and comforting tone that Mary recognised from the first time he had spoken. The soldier continued; "I'm afraid to say I think I stand very little chance of escape." As he spoke he bowed his head, looking down, gesturing towards his legs.

The soldiers right leg seemed twisted painfully at the ankle and he kept his weight on the other foot. For the first time Mary noticed that he was in some pain.

The leg of his airman's jump suit was torn below the knee and in the pale dappled light Mary could see that some blood had stained the cloth from dark green to black.

Realising that she had become completely distracted from her original mission, Mary now quickly helped the soldier over to a nearby straw bale and knelt down beside him, examining the damaged leg.

"Listen. I need to get out of here as quickly as I can. You can't possibly be the only person to see my plane come down."

"I managed to bale out pretty pronto, but it won't take the Jerries long to search the area and track me down. I need to move on – but this blasted ankle is going to be a nuisance." His grimace betrayed the pain he had been hiding.

"Can you help me get fixed up? If I get back home, I promise I'll get word to some of our chaps and we'll see what we can do to get you home. Jerry is desperate and on the run, it won't be long now and the Yanks and Russians will have this all in the bag!"

Mary felt a wave of confidence and resolve sweep over her, could this really be? At the eleventh hour of the war, had a chance to change her life literally landed in her arms?

By helping this brave man, was this her chance to do something good? To make amends for all her youthful stubbornness? To put right her past mistakes?

She met his steely gaze with her own.

"I will help you. But understand that I expect nothing in return. I am at your service and the service of my country. After we have got you fixed up, I'll look after myself."

Hardly believing her own words, she stood and went to retrieve her bundle of provisions.

In a hushed voice from across the room she spoke quickly "I have food and water here. You must be ravenous. I also have some cloths to clean your wound. I suppose we can improvise a bandage from the parachute fabric?"

Mary bandaged his leg and then busied herself fetching bread, meats, cheese and beer. She found herself laying it all out on the floor in a gayish spread, rather like a summer picnic, she thought.

The airman laughed. "Anyone would think we were on Hampstead Heath in the middle of June!"

THE COLDITZ COCK

He slowly lowered himself to the floor and began hurriedly to eat. Mary joined him; for all the world they seemed a couple of young lovers on a romantic adventure.

As they ate they talked. They talked about their families, their childhoods, their dreams for the future.

And as they talked their bodies slowly moved closer to each other until Mary was leaning into her airman, with her arm touching his. As she talked of her dear mother and brother in England, her head slowly came to rest on his shoulder.

As she rested, she sighed. It was the sigh of a woman who, despite being so far from home, had finally found her place. Perhaps this was the home she had been seeking all along?

As the moon outside shone through the cracks in the roof and lit up the scene like a hundred stars, Mary and Freddie, as she discovered he was called, found each other.

They talked and talked, forgetting the danger they were in, forgetting the war raging around them, forgetting the night as it raced towards dawn.

After a time, Freddie reached into his jacket pocket. He drew out a carefully folded piece of paper, worn at the edges and stained by months of close contact to his fatigued body.

"I carry this with me always. It keeps me company through the long nights and days." While he spoke he unfolded the sheet in his hands.

"I was never one for poetry or great literature until this blasted war started," he continued "but something about these words spurs me on. They remind me why we are all in this". He began reading:

> *Cannon to right of them,*
> *Cannon to left of them,*
> *Cannon behind them*
> *Volley'd and thunder'd;*
> *Storm'd at with shot and shell,*

> *While horse and hero fell,*
> *They that had fought so well*
> *Came thro' the jaws of Death*
> *Back from the mouth of Hell,*
> *All that was left of them,*
> *Left of six hundred.*
>
> *When can their glory fade?*
> *O the wild charge they made!*
> *All the world wondered.*
> *Honor the charge they made,*
> *Honor the Light Brigade,*
> *Noble six hundred.*

"Tennyson!" Mary said and smiled as she recognised the author and the poem as one she knew so well.

"'Charge of the Light Brigade'. Such a noble band of men. I admire men of courage who are prepared to fight for what they believe..." When she uttered these words, her eyes locked with his. His beautiful, courageous, deep brown eyes that looked at her now so searchingly.

She was shaken by the force of the feelings that coursed through her body. Barely able to speak she forced the words out of her mouth:

"When I am alone, and this is often, I read Tennyson. Only yesterday, before your unexpected arrival I recited 'Tears, Idle Tears' to myself."

She maintained his gaze and spoke the verses of the poem slowly and deliberately, all the while making the most supreme effort not to cry.

> *Tears, idle tears, I know not what they mean,*
> *Tears from the depth of some divine despair*
> *Rise in the heart, and gather to the eyes,*

> *In looking on the happy Autumn-fields,*
> *And thinking of the days that are no more.*
>
> *Fresh as the first beam glittering on a sail,*
> *That brings our friends up from the underworld,*
> *Sad as the last which reddens over one*
> *That sinks with all we love below the verge;*
> *So sad, so fresh, the days that are no more...*

And with these final words, a single tear began to fall down her cheek, tracing the most beautiful lines of her face and alighted, shining on her lower lip, which trembled with emotion.

"My poor, poor Mary"! My darling, my sweet. How you have suffered. Let me kiss away your tears and your sorrow. He pulled her gently towards him and took her in his arms.

She fell against his warm body and their lips met. Gently and cautiously they kissed as if seeking permission from one another.

Their kisses were soft and almost chaste, with the promise of passion to come.

Mary gave a little sigh of happiness and laid her head against his shoulder. She had found her warrior, a man of whom she could be proud and a love stronger than any she had ever experienced.

But how could this be after one, short night together? Was she fooling herself? Was she looking for a way out of the miserable life she had been enduring? No! She had found love and she must do anything to protect it, to protect him.

Glancing up at the patchwork ceiling Mary noticed that the minute rays of starlight had turned into the dim light of the morning.

At once, she leapt to her feet and began busying herself packing up the remains of their secret picnic.

Freddie joined her as best he could and despite being lame in the right leg, managed expertly to gather and fold away his parachute, hiding it well amongst the bales of straw.

"We must be away," she said "they will surely look for you in here and I will be missed in the house. Heinrich is sleeping off an excess of Nazi brandy and cigars, but he will soon awaken."

She dusted herself down and stood as if to attention. In a businesslike tone she addressed him:

"So where do we go from here?" Mary was noticeably excited and nervous for the new adventure stretching out before her, showing no sign of having not slept one wink of sleep.

"We?" asked Freddie "We aren't going anywhere, my darling," he continued. "Not now. Not together, not today." His firm and abrupt answer surprised her. Since Freddie had first inspired her to action all those hours ago, her life had turned upside down.

Admittedly, she had at first said that once fixed up she would help him escape and then go her own way, alone. But now, having felt his embrace, his kiss, she wasn't ready to say goodbye. Seeing the disappointment and confusion, Freddie explained:

"You must stay here, carry on as if nothing has happened. I will find a way to come back for you, to get you out of this mess and only then can we be together."

His eyes smiled with a roguish twinkle, "no point in us both being wanted by the Reich and behind enemy lines!"

Mary fell to her knees, the promise of love and freedom slipping from her grasp. "You have opened my eyes. I cannot bear another day here. I must come with you."

"Oh, Mary, my love. I am a soldier, an airman. My first duty is to my country. I must get back to England as quickly as possible and having you by my side would increase the danger for both of us."

"We would surely get caught and then what would become of us? You have been safe here till now. I will take the risks for the two of us. And when this is all over, we shall be together, I promise you."

"You promise?" Mary demanded as she moved towards Freddie, cupping his face in her hands.

"My promise is as true as this kiss." His lips met hers and they kissed passionately for the first time. They clung to each other, vibrating to new sensations, new feelings they had never known before.

The pain in her heart subsided a little. For a moment she felt she could fly in the air. "For you I will do this. I will wait here until we can be together. But make me one more promise?"

"Anything my darling."

"You mustn't try to leave this morning. Wait until dusk when there is less chance of anyone seeing you." He nodded in agreement and smiled to himself at her intelligence.

"It will give me a chance to come back at sunset and bring you fresh bread and water. I shall find you some clothes of my husband's too, they will help you pass as a more convincing German!"

In her mind she raced through the rooms of the house, picking out things that would help him escape: "I will find you a pair of boots," she continued. "A gun!" she exclaimed excitedly, "I am sure that there is a hunting gun which no one will miss. There may be some bullets in my husband's study, I am sure I can gain access later on, whilst he is lunching..."

Freddie laughed and pointed at the holster on his belt.

"You know they don't send us into battle completely unarmed!" She blushed at her own naievity.

But Freddie was enchanted at the feisty, clever woman standing in front of him, who only moments ago had seemed paralysed with fear and sorrow.

"I will wait for your return. I'll hide out behind the bales as you ask. It doesn't look as if anyone comes in here." He gestured to the broken machines and abandoned farm tools. "It's as good a hideout as I'll ever find, and with the prettiest neighbours!"

Mary giggled and began to make for the door. She knew that if she didn't seize the moment to leave now, she never would. She blew Freddie a kiss as she turned and stole out into the blanket of morning mist.

Across the grounds she ran, darting between the early morning shadows of the beech trees, confident that she could make it to her bed without being spied by the house staff as they went about their busy routines.

Her husband was easy to evade. He would be sleeping deeply, in that false sleep brought on by alcoholic excess.

Arriving at the house, Mary slowly turned the brass handle of the side door and pushed gently against the heavy, wizened oak.

She squeezed through the smallest of gaps and stood for a moment listening for the slightest sound that would betray the morning stirrings of the house.

She heard nothing. After what was a minute or two, she raised her arm and searched out the small brass light switch on the wall. The metal was cold to her touch. As ever this particular light switch made her smile to herself. She had brought it with her from England and insisted it be installed in the hallway. This type of idiosyncratic behaviour irritated Heinrich and bemused the house staff.

The switch was a quirky gift from another distant admirer. Once on a summer visit with her mother to a country estate, a long standing family friend; Maurice, or Lordy as he was affectionately known to society friends, gave her the switch as a kind of joke saying playfully that Mary was a constant light in dark times.

Lordy was a man of great intelligence and skill of whom Mary was in great awe. He was fascinated by aviation and had even developed his own aircraft. Mary had heard that he had put himself and his skills to great use, testing and flying planes for the Royal Navy.

Lordy could always be trusted to find the most beautifully crafted versions of everyday objects and these light switches were no exception.

It was small and round in shape, but looked rather like the bud of a flower. The switch sat in the middle and she thought it resembled the stamen of a flower.

As she reached for it now, the light flicked into life with a satisfying and almost silent 'click'.

CHAPTER FOUR

It was evening and there was even greater commotion in the house. The family wing of Tatton Park seemed, thought Fenella Layton, to be almost at bursting point.

As the eleventh hour approached, Nell felt it had collided dreadfully with preparations for dinner.

The turmoil of house staff bustling to and fro with trays of food and drinks was now mixing badly with her attempts to hold meetings on matters of war.

"This," thought Nell aloud to herself "is very poor planning indeed!"

"Good evening Nell!" a well–spoken woman's voice came from behind her.

"You made it out of London in one piece I see?" she went on, the tone of her trill voice immediately annoying to Nell. "My husband said, a moment ago, that the newswire is reporting more heavy fire bombing tonight. St Paul's is in flames!" Her voice did not sound concerned, but actually rather excited. Nell was shocked by the news and felt instantly saddened by the countless lives no doubt lost.

Cutting through the Yellow Drawing Room en route to the main War Room, it was Nigel Stalker's insufferable wife Christine.

In one thin hand she held a Champagne flute, half emptied. The other arm, over which her handbag was slung, held what appeared to Nell to be a dish containing devilled eggs. Nell's dislike of Christine and her greedy husband was carefully concealed by a business–like expression of neutrality.

Fortunately, the intolerable Christine did not stop to exchange more news. This was greatly to Nell's relief.

She now turned to continue her admiration of the many oil paintings that hung on the walls.

However, no sooner had she turned away than she was greeted by another voice.

"There you are my dear." It was Charlie, she too was carrying Champagne, this time two glasses.

"Would you like a drink?" She proffered one to Nell, who declined.

"This is supposed to be a serious evening of planning!" she thought slightly angrily to herself, "Why on earth was everyone treating the event as a party?" Her famous patience was being tried.

However, in hurrying to judgement, Nell had not noticed the sadness apparent in Charlie's eyes.

She looked more attentively now.

Had she been crying? Surely not! Something had clearly upset Charlie since Nell had last seen her several hours ago.

Nell was no sleuth, but recent discoveries made unexpectedly during the recent highly pressured weeks in Downing Street, gave her plenty of clues as to why her friend might feel dejected.

"Do you think I could have a few words?" She leaned close to Nell as she spoke. "In private, if you're not too busy?"

"No, not at all." answered Nell. "I was only waiting for your husband, to escort him to the War Room for our next session. I'm supposed to record everything," she continued. "I believe he's still in the bathroom."

As Nell spoke, Charlie's face seemed to fall. The mention of her husband the Prime Minister, made her look suddenly as if she was on the edge of some kind of minor breakdown.

Nell thought quickly and realised that she must act fast to save the deteriorating situation.

Events must have gotten worse than she had suspected.

It was time to act and act decisively she must.

The war effort was hanging by a thread and the Prime Minister's wife was needed by his side. Nell knew instinctively that it was her and her alone that held the keys to victory.

"Now, let's find a quiet place to talk." Nell took Charlie's slender and beautiful arm gently and the two walked together into a tiny side room, where they would not be disturbed.

It was a closet of sorts and there was no obvious light switch.

After fumbling around for a few moments, Nell's fingers discovered a small brass switch and flicked it on.

They were in fact in a walk–in closet, there was nowhere to sit, only shelves of dusty old books and some spare linen in a glass cabinet on the wall.

The light shone brightly on the yellow dress and attractive face of Charlie. She seemed proud and not the kind of woman who would be easily upset. Her lips trembled as she spoke and the two glasses she still clutched trembled also.

"My dear friend, I know how close you are to my husband, but something dreadful has occurred and I must confide in someone."

"Promise me with all your heart that you will not divulge a single word of what I am about to tell you." She reinforced her point; "please understand, what I tell you must never leave this closet."

"Of course Charlie." She hoped that speaking her friend's name, rather than using something more familiar or affectionate such as 'darling' or 'dear' would maintain some distance between them and preserve some air of professionalism.

Nell was, after all, in her husband's employment. She was stealing herself now for a revelation, although she had a fairly good idea of what Charlie was about to confide in her.

THE COLDITZ COCK

Charlie appeared to be getting increasingly upset.

"Nell, I caught him earlier. The cheating fool!" exclaimed a now fraught Charlie

"Whatever do you mean?" Nell thought it prudent not to let slip in her reactions that she, along with most of the Prime Minister's private staff, suspected that he was 'playing away'. Power and the riches that are associated with gaining it, seem to both corrupt and attract the weak, thought Nell privately.

She listened patiently as the revelation unfolded in all its sordid detail.

"I walked in on them earlier, while you were upstairs." Charlie was shaking with emotion. "Another woman! In his arms."

"Who do you mean?" Nell's mind worked quickly through the possibilities. Who had they brought with them from London? The Prime Minister's entourage was enormous.

"It wasn't anyone I thought it would be," sniffed Charlie through the tears which had escaped down her pretty cheek.

"It's a silly little maid from Tatton, of all people!" She was as angry as she was upset.

"I should have guessed when I noticed the way she looked at him when he arrived, the strumpet!"

"What's her name? Which girl?" enquired Nell quietly, touching Charlie on the arm in an act of sisterly comfort.

She didn't need to know, this was not a matter of national security, she thought, but now the story was out, her inquisitiveness had got the better of her. Private Secretary she might be, but Nell considered herself to be above such gossip.

"Edwina." Charlie spat out the name as if Nell would recognise who she meant.

Nell did not, but tried nevertheless to scour her memories from previous visits.

"She's part of the kitchen staff." Charlie clarified.

"I caught them in the store just now, when I was bringing

that cheat a glass of Champagne!"

The tears now flowed freely, blurring Charlie's perfectly mascarered lashes. Holding the two glasses, she had no way to stem the flow of tears.

"I know it's not a good time, but I so wanted this stay at Tatton to bring us closer together."

"When we are apart and our private life is, you know..." she stopped to sniff, "just, a little cold..." She paused and fixed Nell with her weeping eyes.

Nell knew exactly what Charlie was alluding to. She listened patiently.

Charlie now spoke with pride and Nell recognised again the strength in this woman, how hard she had struggled in a world of men, and how she had fought to overturn their petty prejudices!

Outside of her professional life and Downing Street, Charlie was very much the darling of the tabloids.

Her clothes were made especially for her and copied by every high street department store.

She was viewed as strong and admirable by ordinary people of the middle and lower classes, who quite rightly looked up to her.

She was a paragon of virtue to most, a fighter for justice, who championed the rights of midwives and gypsy children in her charity work.

To see her now, reduced to tears, ripped through Nell.

She could not stand by and watch this woman lose standing through the sordid actions of her husband.

"I really thought I could turn our relationship around, make him notice me more and maybe it would give him new vigour, help him focus on his work." Nell thought how typical it was of a woman like her, to think of the country and others before herself.

Nell wanted at that moment to be just as brave.

The two women stood silently together for a moment under the bare lightbulb.

From behind the wall they could hear the muffled sounds of the men arguing endlessly about 'troop carriers' and 'stretched supply lines'.

Nell looked at Charlie and smiled unexpectedly. Charlie looked back confused, the tears drying on her cheeks.

It was time for Nell to put her plan to save her Prime Minister into action.

She took the spare glass of fizzing Champagne from Charlie's hand and sipped at it once, placing it on the bookshelf.

"We girls should stick together," she said as she reached into her blazer pocket for a handkerchief.

"I have just the thing to fix this." This was her standard response to any crisis, whatever its dimensions.

As Charlie gratefully used Nell's handkerchief to wipe away her tears, Nell left the closet.

She was caught completely unawares as she re-entered the Drawing Room by the presence of Baron Egerton; 'Lordy'.

Apparently he had been waiting outside the closet for her, but for how long, she could not determine.

CHAPTER FIVE

The light came on and there, looming over her was Heinrich.

As her eyes became accustomed to the light, they focussed on his face. Was it anger, disappointment or betrayal that she read in his expression?

"Where, in the name of love, have you been?" He grasped the hand that still hovered above the light switch. Mary sensed that he was perhaps a little drunk.

"I... I... needed air," she stammered "I thought a walk would clear my..."

"No Mary, please," he exclaimed, "please do not lie to me. I returned home early and realised immediately that you were not in your room." Heinrich continued, "I was worried and I have been looking for you everywhere." The tone of his voice was sad rather than angry, as if he had suffered a great disappointment.

He must have seen her as she returned to the house across the lawn, betrayed by the rising sun. Clearly he had been waiting behind the door for her to try to enter undetected.

"Heinrich. Why do you question me so?" Mary searched desperately for a plausible reason to justify her absence from the house. How could she explain this away? She could barely explain it to herself!

Freddie had literally fallen into her life 24 hours ago, and here she was, lying to her husband's concerned face, betraying him.

"I was missing my family so," she offered a half truth by way of explanation, "but I didn't want to trouble you. I know how you fret about me." She paused, waiting to see if her husband would buy her excuse.

A quick study of his reaction told Mary that Heinrich was not buying anything.

Heinrich knew her well enough to see that although his wife did miss her home in England, this was not the reason for her stealing out alone under the cover of darkness. He was certain there was more to this than met the eye.

As he looked down at her, Heinrich's sadness at her deceit slowly began to transform into something akin to irritation.

"I don't believe you Mary. I don't know why you cannot be truthful with me. What is it? What has happened? Are you in trouble? In danger? Tell me now please, where have you been?"

His eyes searched her face for answers. There was a long silence and under the interrogation of his masterful relentless stare, Mary realised she did not stand much of a chance.

She had been brought up too well and lying was something to which she was not accustomed. Against every ounce of her will and despite such a strong desire to protect her newly budding love, Mary's resolve collapsed, this was all too much for her. She felt herself beginning to crumble.

"Oh Heinrich!" she cried. "I am so sorry. It wasn't meant to happen. I didn't plan any of this. You are a good man. I never intended to put us in danger. But we are in danger now, terrible danger and I need your help."

Heinrich stood in total shock. "For heaven's sake, Mary, what have you gone and done?" he demanded.

Heinrich's irritation was transforming into anger before her very eyes. For a lady to disobey her husband was surely inexcusable, but for a noble, a Baroness no less, it was a crime he could not allow to go unpunished.

As she backed away from him, his arm reached out and grabbed her roughly, tightly, by the wrist.

They stood, frozen in a moment that they would both remember for the rest of their lives. She was suddenly once again at Heinrich's mercy and felt instinctively that the game was up.

"Last night, after you left, an airman bailed out over our house and landed in the grounds," she began cautiously, in an almost confessional whisper.

Her husband, the Baron, began noticeably to seethe with fury. This was worse than he had expected.

"Heinrich I... I did not know what to do! You were not here so I went out alone and I discovered him hiding out in..." she halted.

She could not quite bring herself even now to reveal Freddie's hiding place.

Heinrich grabbed her other wrist and shook her roughly, "Are you quite mad, woman?" he exclaimed.

"I discovered him hiding out in another part of the grounds," she continued "The man was injured, gravely injured. I could not leave him there suffering. Oh Heinrich! I did not stay with him for very long. I was so afraid."

She had confessed to the meeting, but resolved to never tell the whole story, her new-found love, the stolen kiss, no matter how hard her husband pushed, Mary would not tell the whole tale.

"Where is this man hiding Mary?" Heinrich now shouted in a fury, "tell me at once! I demand to know!"

Mary held her tongue.

"What has become of him? Where is he now?" Heinrich was so close to her now that she could smell his anger. Still she did not reply, but steadied herself instead for the consequences, for what she feared would certainly happen if Heinrich did not get a satisfactory answer.

In the few years that Mary had been his wife, the Baron had never struck out at her, but she had seen him on occasion lash out at the poor lad who used to tend their horses.

Certainly his reputation in the village was of a man who got what he asked for and would use his strength if necessary to get it.

"I will not ask again; what has become of this man? You must tell me or we are both guilty of harbouring an enemy of The Reich!"

As those last two words left his twisted mouth Heinrich drew back his hand and slapped her on one side of the face, then on the other.

The impact of his hand was extremely painful, but Mary's pride did not let her wince away or even cry out.

She stood there facing her husband, her cheeks beginning to burn from the blows, but her eyes were quite steady.

They stood, face to face and it was as if a vast chasm had opened up between them and they could neither walk around it or step over it.

Mary spoke calmly, trying to appease Heinrich, without actually betraying Freddie's location. She began again.

"You weren't here when I first discovered him and I must have lost track of the time. It was frightfully scary for me, but I could not leave a countryman of mine alone, suffering in the dark."

Like a gun dog Heinrich seized on these words. "Ha! A countryman! So, he is British!" He turned sharply away and this time it was Mary who grabbed at Heinrich's arm, catching him desperately by the hand as he stepped away. The coldness of his skin came as a surprise to her.

"British, yes. British" she repeated again, almost inaudibly.

"So now we know where your allegiance really lies," replied Heinrich. "You disappoint me. Not only have you betrayed my trust and disobeyed my explicit order to remain indoors to preserve your safety, but you acted in a way which could ruin my position here."

Heinrich began to pace the room, hands clasped behind his back, thinking aloud.

"You have put our peaceful life here in dire jeopardy! Have you no idea what I have to go through to keep the secret police from our door? Imagine how you have brought shame to my house, what if news of this stupid mistake of yours reached the village... or the city? My word, what if news that my wife was a conspirator reached Berlin?"

He span about on his heels. The rage in him was now being overtaken by genuine fear, both emotions now contorting his face in equal proportion.

Mary slumped lifelessly and exhausted into a chair, her mind racing to find a solution to her dreadful predicament. Heinrich for his part continued to pace ever more angrily about the parlour.

Mary found herself beginning to think harder than she ever had before.

Although the train of events that she had set in motion careened dangerously out of control, despite her husband's fury and her stinging face, Mary began to see that a way out of this was becoming apparent.

"I did not mean to anger you, or put either of us in danger. You know how impulsive I can be," she spoke cautiously.

"I admit, I really didn't think any of this through to its logical conclusion, I simply couldn't bear to see someone hurt, alone and suffering. He was like a poor, injured bird falling from the sky."

Heinrich was by the window now, across the room, motionless. Mary swallowed hard and continued.

"I'm so very sorry for the trouble I have caused." she said, "What if we just pretend this never happened? I promise you I will not mention it to anyone, ever."

Heinrich began to pace again and Mary spoke faster,

careful not to loose the headway she felt she was now making.

"We can forget this man ever existed and no one need know about it, here or in Berlin. We can start over, my darling."

"I will never disobey you or stray from the castle again. Please?" Her question hung in the still air of the morning parlour. The only noise was Heinrich's boots on the parquet.

Then quite suddenly Heinrich stopped in mid-stride and the room fell silent.

Was he really about to forgive her? Could he ignore this whole episode and walk away, his reputation as a loyal Party member, head of the house and a strict husband intact? There was no doubting her logic, if she could be made to keep the encounter with the airman a secret.

"Very well." Heinrich's mind was made up.

"We will leave this wounded dog to his fate. Hopefully he will already be gone from his sorry hiding hole, wherever that might be." He shot a stare across the room at Mary, who in response stared a hole deep into the pink fabric of the chaise.

"Not a word of this event or conversation will ever leave this castle and for the time being, neither will you!" Heinrich approached Mary as she sat, until he was towering over her.

"I will not be informing the SS," he spoke quietly now, close to her face which still bore the red marks of his hand, "and the price for my forgiveness and leniency is this: you will never disobey me again, so long as you are my wife. Do you understand?"

Mary did not answer, but Heinrich must have taken her silence as a 'yes'.

As he left the room and shut the door, Mary let out a sigh.

At least what had really happened that night had not been completely revealed, she thought. Her night of love and desire for Freddie had not been discovered and most importantly the location of the hidden airman remained a mystery. Although in reality she was trapped again, in her heart she was still free.

Mary breathed out another long sigh of relief as she thought of Freddie in the barn. What had happened would never be erased. She might have to wait longer than she had at first desired, but she knew her own mind finally. She was sure Heinrich would not go looking for Freddie; his social standing could not be risked. With any luck he was right, that Freddie would be able to make good his escape and one day, perhaps after the war, Mary would find a way to escape too, her marriage, the castle and Germany.

She stood slowly and walked to the window and looked out across the lake. Perhaps, she thought, hers and Freddie's paths would one day meet again.

. . . . .

Mary retired to her room. She took off yesterday's clothes, peeling away the trauma of the last twenty-four hours, layer by layer.

Gisela drew her a bath and she lay, motionless, replaying events through her exhausted brain.

Downstairs, the household was going about its daily business as usual.

There was no reason for it to be otherwise; the staff were certainly unaware of the stranger in their midst and her argument with Heinrich.

And so it must remain. However loyal and trusting the relationship between Mary and her staff, she would never confide in them.

It was well known how servants were not to be trusted and anyway, thought Mary, it was unfair to raise false expectation by treating them as equals. In this household as in all others, everyone knew their place and what was expected of them.

Mary concluded, as she lay there in the warm water, that whatever affection she felt for Gisella and Gerta, she was still very much alone and friendless.

Mary listened to the comforting sounds drifting in from the kitchen and they must have lulled her to sleep.

She awoke with a start, some time later. The water had cooled, so Mary rang for Gisella who brought her a fresh towel and helped her out of the tub.

As she dressed, Mary enquired casually after her husband; "have you seen Heinrich today? I can't remember what was in his diary? Has he gone into town?"

"I'm not sure madam", she replied "he has been gone since you started to take your bath. He took the Stabswagen, so I presume so."

This eased Mary's mind. If her husband had taken the car and was going about his business as usual, then everything was as it should be and Freddie was still safe.

At the thought of Freddie, Mary could not resist glancing towards the barn out of the misted window. She pressed her hand against the glass, leaving the imprint of her delicate fingers on the pane.

Now that their escape had been thwarted, Mary could see no chance of happiness for them. He would remain in her heart forever, and the one night they had spent together would be with her always.

There was little she could do now. If she went to him again, she would surely be putting both herself and him in grave danger. She would have to obey her husband and it was a risk she simply couldn't take.

Mary knew that she needed to busy herself for the rest the day until Heinrich returned. Then she would have the long and perhaps fruitless task of beginning to carve out a new existence for herself by his side.

It would be an existence without love, and perhaps without happiness. But it would be a safe haven until the war was over.

Britain would surely win the war! A German victory was not conceivable. That would mean certain destitution for the Von Strauss family, but her friends in England would see her safe and Heinrich too, no doubt.

CHAPTER SIX

The long day dragged into afternoon. Mary busied herself reading.
Although the library seemed at a glance to be a very comprehensive one, she personally found it wanting somewhat, suffering in the most part from not being entirely in her native tongue and also from Heinrich's slightly impoverished imagination.

The books made her feel as if she had travelled to many places in her imagination. She knew of peoples and places that she was well aware she would never have the chance of meeting or seeing.

She carefully avoided picking up the works of Tennyson, unsure that her heart could endure that pain!

But she read some works by Dylan Thomas that had been sent to her before the war by her brother in England.

The works she read spoke of nature, the sea and not of love. This distracted her heart sufficiently that the arrival of afternoon tea surprised her somewhat.

Gerta served a small plate of scones with jam and butter. Heinrich's black market dealings kept their larder properly stocked.

Gerta was rightly proud of her baking skills and had been keen to learn new recipes from Mary when she arrived at the house.

For her part, Mary had been delighted to have a little piece of home provided to her on a delicate china plate every day, and had carefully tutored Gerta in getting the consistency and shape just right.

Not that Mary had vast experience of getting her hands dirty in a kitchen; but from years of taking tea at society gatherings, she knew precisely how afternoon tea should be served.

Oh! How they had whiled away hours conversing about the arts, politics and the fashions of the day before the war. How she missed talking and laughing with friends; there was no one here with whom she could really laugh. Germans didn't seem to share the British love for amusing anecdotes, witticisms and puns.

She tried to think of the last time she had really laughed. And then that memory came back to her so strongly that she had to catch her breath.

It had been last night, in the barn, with him. She had giggled so much she had hardly been able to speak. It was Freddie that had made her smile so.

Putting down her china cup carefully on the side table, she sat back and closed her eyes. The image of his face shone inside her head.

Try as she might, the image would not dissolve. His beautiful, noble face was imprinted as if it had been burned into her very being.

"Oh, it is of no use!" she almost shouted aloud. "I must go to him. I promised him I would bring fresh dressings! I cannot betray him or the love that I know we share."

"How can I sit here obediently, while he suffers?"

She stood now and moved towards the door.

"I cannot deny him the chance to live, or deny my true feelings. I must be brave."

And without a second thought and in complete defiance of her husband, she opened her bedroom door and stole down to the kitchen below.

She found the kitchen full of heat and noise and so Mary

decided instead to make straight for the store room.

Gerta was so occupied with dinner that she did not notice her mistress approaching, nor leaving the store shortly after with a small bundle.

The bundle contained basic supplies, just as it had the night before.

Mary dressed herself in her outdoor coat and shoes, over the top of a simple muslin she had run up for herself a few weeks previously. It was tied about the waist with a blue scarf which she had kept since she was a child.

Coat collar turned up, she carefully unlocked the side door to the house and headed out into the gardens.

There was no one about and the car her husband used to visit his business associates and contacts in the village was not in its usual place. Although this meant Heinrich was nowhere to be found, "I must hurry," she thought, "if I want to get to Freddie and back before he returns."

She tried to walk calmly, but her feet carried her forward quickly; in her mind she could not wait to prove to Freddie that she had not forsaken him and of course to be with him again, to hold him one more time.

She turned at the corner of the field by the trees, from where she had last night approached the barnyard. From this concealed vantage point she stopped to survey the last few yards to the barn. It was lucky that she did.

In clear view, not a stone's throw from where she now stood petrified, an army truck and a staff car, no doubt from the prison on the hill, were parked right in front of the barn door.

As she took in the scene, with unbelieving eyes Freddie appeared, limping and restrained between two soldiers, who seemed to Mary to be mere boys.

"He must have been captured! But how? We were right to assume his crashing plane would not go unnoticed!"

A sudden commotion caused Mary to move forward, almost revealing her hiding place.

Freddie had managed to break free and seemed to be making his way as fast as his injured leg would carry him, towards her position.

"Run to me, run my love!" she silently urged him on. But it was to no avail.

The young soldiers reached for their pistols. As they tried to take aim, Freddie ducked and made for cover behind the cab of the truck.

Just as he was almost clear a man darted out from nowhere and tackled Freddie to the ground. Standing up with Freddie lifeless at his feet, the tall, muscular man dusted himself down. It was Heinrich!

It was only now that Mary recognised the other car at the scene; it wasn't a staff car from the prison, but Heinrich's own black Stabswagen. He had double-crossed her. The fiend!

Rooted to the spot in absolute disbelief, Mary watched in horror as the soldiers hauled up Freddie's lifeless broken body and dragged it to the open back of the truck. Heinrich followed close behind, dusting down his khaki jodhpurs, a satisfied look on his chiselled face.

As the soldiers heaved Freddie into the truck, Heinrich stepped forward and gave him a swift kick in his injured leg.

"There'll be no more running away for you", he proclaimed loudly for all to hear, as if seeking recognition for his capture.

The Commandant, who had sat all the while smoking in Heinrich's car, now joined the group. He slapped Heinrich conspiratorially on the back and congratulated him; "ah Heinrich, I see you are as fast as ever! Perhaps we should call you up!"

Heinrich laughed uneasily and retorted, "well, we both know I am more use to you in other ways, like keeping my ear to the ground and sniffing out traitors." He gestured to the truck, "I'm always happy to bring you new inmates!"

The two men laughed together, then turned to watch as the truck began to pull away. The road from the barn skirted the lower field and Mary withdrew slightly into the shadows as it approached.

Her head was burning with hatred for Heinrich, for his betrayal and for the needless cruelty she had witnessed.

Freddie's broken face was visible from the back of the truck as it passed her by. She leaned forward, risking discovery, to see if he was alive or dead.

She looked straight at him, trying with all her being to tell him with her eyes that it had not been her who had betrayed him.

He looked straight at her and in that one tiny moment, though bruised and battered, he understood.

Her expression of devotion, that bundle in her hands; his angel had not forsaken or betrayed him.

He summoned a smile and she smiled back. Mary watched until she could see his face and the truck no more.

. . . . . .

Stepping out of the car at dusk, Mary and Heinrich were faced at once by the imposing image of the prison, Oflag IV–C or, as it was known throughout the world, Colditz Castle.

Looming above the rest of the landscape and set high above the town on a rocky hilltop, the endless whitewashed stone of the south perimeter wall took on a ghostly quality in the moonlight.

"I wish we didn't have to do this," Mary said, turning to her husband Heinrich as he helped her down.

For Mary, her carefully chosen words had added meaning.

Since the capture and disappearance of Freddie and the revelation of her husband's complicity in it, Mary had found herself forced into an uncomfortable truce with Heinrich.

She had stayed loyal and played the part of the dutiful wife as her family and society expected, but every day found herself dreaming up new ways of escaping her predicament.

"Please don't complain Mary, you know what a difficult position I am in," spoke Heinrich coldly. "When the Commandant asks you to come for dinner, you do not keep him waiting, especially if he is your cousin."

Wherever Heinrich and Mary had visited in Europe under the Nazi Reich, they seemed to have encountered exceptionally comfortable members of the Von Strauss branch of German aristocracy.

They appeared to have fitted themselves in very snugly behind the jackbooted invaders, gobbling up resources and lording over the poor natives.

Mary found them to be most risible in every way and had concluded long ago that Saxony aristocracy was inferior to the English and that the spoils of war had not made them nicer people to dine with.

A line of German soldiers greeted them with the cool air of rigid contempt that was their default position when greeting even civilian visitors.

"Good evening Baron Von Strauss," the senior officer said with a weak smile. "Welcome to Colditz, the Commandant is expecting you in his quarters. Please follow me."

Mary noticed that the officer did not welcome her personally. He merely flashed again his false smile and turned on his heels sharply to lead them into the castle.

Hitler's appreciation of English Aristocracy was not automatically shared by all Germany.

The respect and popularity which Mary had experienced as an English Lady growing up in London society, was another thing she had taken for granted at home, which had been stripped of her on arrival in Saxony.

Her title and marriage into the Von Strauss lineage had only seemed to compound their distrust of her.

Mary felt the eyes of every soldier on her as she walked by and suddenly felt exposed and vulnerable in her thin silk evening gown.

Shifting the fur shawl that covered her bare shoulders, as if it were a protective shield, she moved forward through a tall fence adorned with huge quantities of menacing barbed wire.

. . . . .

Colditz Castle housed many of the Allied Forces' most notorious prisoners of war, including compulsive escapists, forgers, locksmiths and engineers that the Germans felt were too high risk to keep anywhere else.

The number of attempted escapes from the castle was famed across Europe and for many of the prisoners, getting out was their one and only mission.

Knowing of the legendary prisoners at the castle, the level of security in the Entry House's dark tunnel was unsettling but came as no surprise to Mary, who tried her best to remain calm as her bag was checked by a particularly oafish soldier.

"Really!" thought Mary to herself. "Such an indignity."

Crossing under the ornate renaissance-style façade Mary was ushered through by another host of solders in starched green uniforms and metallic domed helmets.

Finding herself thrust out onto a cobbled bridge that straddled the imposing dry moat Mary's eyes adjusted to the moonlight, and the terrifying scale of Colditz's tiered terraces as they reared up in front of her.

Two giant flags adorned with the swastika of the Nazi

Party covered the front of the monumental clock tower. They cast a foreboding eye upon her along with the rest the city.

While Mary was now used to seeing these swaths of nationalistic crimson and black silk all over the Rhineland, tonight it felt suffocating. Although it was still late summer in the valley, Mary felt herself shiver involuntarily.

Swallowing down any feelings of fear, Mary held her head up high and strode through the Castle's main entrance, knowing that her ability to survive in this hostile environment depended on her wits alone.

Heinrich was striding confidently by her side, looking the very part, but she had learned over the previous months not only not to rely on his protection, but to mistrust him and fear him constantly.

Entering the Commandanture's courtyard, Mary and her husband were greeted by several of the high-ranking officers including the Commandant, Lieutenant Colonel Prawitt, a tall hard faced man, who had obviously already been drinking with his guests.

"Good evening and welcome, dear cousin!" the Commandant roared, slapping Heinrich on the back.

Heinrich stepped back and snapped to attention, performing a salute, something which Mary had never seen him do before. Was it a joke? The Commandant did laugh out loud.

Heinrich relaxed his stance and joined in the laughter; "it's good to see you, thank you for your kind invitation Hans, we are honoured." replied Heinrich.

The Commandant turned to face Mary and smiled thinly.

Mary bowed gently to each of the officers before extending a gloved hand to the Commandant himself, who kissed it gently and looked her up and down with a look of mischievous contempt.

"Welcome to Colditz Frau," the Commandant said loudly so all could hear, "I do hope you enjoy your time with us this evening; I'm sure you will appreciate our German hospitality."

"I understand you have one the best pastry chiefs in all of the Rhine here; I do hope he will be cooking for us this evening," Mary retorted confidently.

Satisfied by the banality and submissive nature of her reply the Commandant responded, "you have heard correctly my dear, I'm certain there will be a delicacy or two for you to try, so let us go inside!"

Mary had decided her mission tonight was to maintain a low profile; she hoped that with polite chatter about food and entertainment she could avoid nationalist politics and talk of the war.

She and her husband were quickly led towards a door at the east of the courtyard where the party was to be held in the Commandant's private quarters.

But suddenly, before Mary could enter the doorway, there was a roar of noise from above.

Stopping to understand what the outburst was, the group looked up instinctively and their escort of guards grabbed at their rifles.

Surprised at what she saw, Mary looked up to see the faces of several dozen British soldiers being held captive in the upper floors of the castle.

Many shouted mockingly at the group of German guards, while others clattered tin cups against the bars of the windows.

"They shouldn't take their privileges for granted," remarked the Commandant to Heinrich as he continued without so much as a glance upwards.

"With the war going the way it is, less lenient men could arrive tomorrow with orders to liquidate this place."

As guards were dispatched to quell the upsurge Mary kept quiet knowing that drawing attention to herself now would only cause problems. She too hurried along and into the Commandanture.

Below her cool façade Mary was secretly elated. To her, hearing the language of her homeland was a welcome reprise from the relentless harshness of barked German orders that seemed to surround her these days.

. . . .

In stark contrast to the austerity of the castle's courtyard, the Commandant's private quarters were somewhat palatial.

The smell of cooked meats and fine cigars filled the air as Mary entered the candlelit dinning room where all of the guests were busy talking noisily over one another about the politics of the day.

In each corner of the room a German soldier stood perfectly to attention, as the newly arrived guests found their seats at the long mahogany table.

"So, cousin," the Commandant addressed Heinrich after he finished settling in his chair and unfolding a napkin, "I have not had the opportunity to congratulate you on the dramatic capture you made the other week!"

"It has been the talk of the barracks and I believe the village too since word got around."

"Those British flying aces have been causing a lot of problems for our Luftwaffe boys over the last few months," he reached for his glass and continued, "it must feel good to get a little revenge?"

"No, no, Commandant," Heinrich replied, "it was nothing, the man just fell into my lap!"

The pair roared with laughter and the Commandant slapped his cousin firmly on the arm before raising his crystal glass in a toast.

"To the broken wing of the RAF and victory to the

Luftwaffe!" he cheered and swallowed down the remaining wine.

Heinrich followed suit and drank from his own glass laughing heartily without so much as a glance towards Mary next to him.

If anything, Heinrich seemed pleased that his part in the capture of Freddie had proved his loyalty to the Commandant and, feeling like the hero of the hour, he began to relax into the evening.

Mary sat across the table from her husband and quietly seethed. How could they mock her country and the man she had loved?

While on the outside she smiled genially at the conversation that rattled around her, inside all she could think about was Freddie and what could have become of him. She dare not ask!

As the evening wore on, Mary found herself slipping off into a sort of daydream, reminiscing about that one night that she had spent with Freddie in the barn.

She longed to feel him close to her once more, to hear his voice as he read their beloved Tennyson aloud and to perhaps run her fingers through his hair.

Amid the clatter of cutlery and laughter she once again felt so alone and betrayed; trapped in a country where she constantly lived in fear, with nobody that she could trust.

Looking up she surveyed the room that buzzed around her and noticed that dinner was now being served.

Six thin and rather elegant waiters in starched white linen placed bowls of pale, somewhat lumpy looking soup in front of each guest, who for their part continued to chatter, or in the case of the Commandant and his fellow officers, compete loudly for the whole table's attention.

Heinrich was deep in conversation with the guests beside him and Mary was completely disengaged from the party.

She privately studied the quiet and deliberate movements of the servers and their concentrating faces in more detail.

They seemed excellently trained and reminded her somewhat of being waited upon at a rather excellent house–party she had once attended with her mother at Tranby Croft in Yorkshire.

Such quality of service is really only found in the grandest English or Scottish country houses.

It was only at that point that Mary remembered a conversation she'd had with Gerta one afternoon recently and realised that often the more suitable prisoners of war held in the castle were used as servants and waiters.

Mary's heart fluttered as she understood that these men were indeed British: their skin tone and familiar bone structure at once confirmed it to her. Suddenly she was back home and in the familiar company of friends.

She allowed her eyes to close momentarily and Mary imagined herself in a fine English restaurant; in her dream the war was a distant memory and she was happy again.

The arm of her own waiter reached to her right and placed a bowl of soup in front of her.

Instantly she recognised the hand, the fine, long fingers. Was she in her dream or back at the Commandant's dinner? Surely it couldn't be that one of the prisoners serving her now was Freddie?

She dared not believe it, or hope that it could be true. Could he be alive, and right here next to her at that very moment?

To turn and look at him now would be too dangerous, as she would melt with joy.

Before Mary could decide how to react, the waiter's arm reached for the linen napkin and placed it across her lap, as was the custom in the high establishments and restaurants of the day.

And with that he was gone.

Her heart felt as if it were in her mouth and her hands were shaking so violently that she had to place them underneath the table on her lap to hide them from the rest of the dinner party.

It was at that moment that Mary felt something amongst the soft cotton of her napkin.

Allowing her eyes to dart quickly around the room, she checked that the other guests were absorbed in their food and dinner talk, and satisfied, she took the chance to glance down at the object in her hands.

What she saw was a small white piece of paper folded many times in on itself. She concealed the note quickly in her small trembling hand, barely able to dream of what it might contain.

"Are you not enjoying your Bavarian liver dumpling soup?" the Commandant asked Mary suddenly.

Realising that she had not touched her food Mary clutched tightly at the hidden note now in her possession and with her other hand she picked up the silver spoon to begin.

Taking just a few small sips of the soup, she replaced the spoon on the plate.

"I'm sorry Commandant, I'm afraid that I am still just feeling a little shaken up about the little incident with the prisoners in the courtyard earlier."

She hoped this small lie would conceal her obvious surprise at the incredible encounter with a man until moments before she was convinced was dead.

It had to have been Freddie, very much alive and trying to contact her.

"I wouldn't worry," said the Commandant, "the prisoners are quite under control," he went on. "And anyway, there is no need to conceal your feelings."

Mary's heart jumped to her throat as she listened. The

CARTLAND INSTITUTE FOR ROMANCE RESEARCH

Commandant laughed as he spoke.

"Not every Englishwoman, no matter how well bred, can conceal her dislike of the liver dumpling!"

Mary breathed again as Heinrich and the other guests laughed loudly at their host's joke.

"Would you gentlemen excuse me." Mary said, seeing this as the only opportunity she was going to have to be alone and to read the note she held tightly in her palm.

"Please, feel free, my staff will direct you to the bathrooms. Unless it is the chef and the kitchens you need to seek?"

As Mary left the room, she could hear the Commandant and her husband laughing at her expense, but she was too preoccupied by the contents of the note she carried to take any offense.

CHAPTER SEVEN

"Have you seen the PM?" asked a well-educated voice.

"Lordy!" Nell exclaimed, racing across the room and carefully side–stepping the question.

As she held her arms wide to the waiting gentleman, she asked warmly "How long it has been?"

"You look as beautiful as ever, Nell!" said Lordy, kissing her hand and bowing slightly. "Welcome back to Tatton Park, you must tell me all the news from London."

The two had begun to talk as though neither had ever left the other's company.

"I'm afraid," replied Nell, "that our beloved capital is not what it once was." Her expression was grim and instantly business–like, as she informed her old friend of the situation.

"The Nazi bombs have decimated much of what we treasure. But I trust you have been safe, the Luftwaffe has not targeted these remote parts of the Kingdom so heavily?"

"We do see the occasional bombing raid, en route to Liverpool, yes. And the skies are alight with firestorms every night. But we are all largely intact and pulling together for the big push." Nell nodded sombrely.

"And it is to this matter which you must immediately turn your attention and experience." Lordy's face was hard to read. He was evidently serious, but there was something else hidden behind his eyes.

"I know, dear friend," Nell continued. "I was trying to co-ordinate another meeting when I was distracted."

Lordy's face broke into a broad and rather cheeky smile.

"I won't ask what the two of you were conspiring about in the linen cupboard!" He laughed.

Behind her Nell became aware that the Prime Minister's wife had just emerged from the closet.

"Sorry, I don't mean to interrupt." said Charlie in a clear and unashamed voice. She left the room with several books and a folded linen bed sheet in her arms.

"How extraordinary!" quipped Lordy to Nell, raising an eyebrow. Nell ignored his mischievous attempts to elicit gossip. There was work to do.

At that very moment the sound of voices began to emanate from the other side of the room. A door opened in a panelled wall and several earnest looking Cabinet aides entered the Drawing Room with bundles of papers and maps under their arms.

"Madame. Sir," spoke the oldest of the men from over his glasses as he addressed the pair. "We have been waiting for you."

"Do you have The Prime Minister with you?" asked Nell.

"The Prime Minister has been briefed by the Generals and the military staff has just arrived from Bletchley" came the reply. "Do come this way."

Nell spent the next four or so hours in the most dramatic and hectic of meetings. Even after such long and intense discussion, the Cabinet was unconvinced that the next wave of invasion operations was ready to proceed.

The difficulty was not strength of forces, with the Americans poised for action and their transports requisitioned for the big push. Disagreements instead surrounded speed of deployment and supply routes.

Reports had come in from spies in the field and these were now shared around the table, along with intelligence gathered by code–breakers at Bletchley.

Every shred of evidence showed that the Germans were

hopelessly stretched along the Siegfried Line and under heavy bombardment.

As a result of this news, morale on the side of the Allies was, in the eyes of Nell, sailing dangerously high.

Nell knew something of the RAF and its capacity for troop deployment. Aeronautical engineering and aviation in general was in her family's blood.

As the talking and arguing over maps dragged on into the night, she began to quietly despair.

"Oh why?" she quietly whispered to Lordy, who was sat beside her poring over acres of transcribed radio reports and page upon page of numbers which Nell took to be encryption codes or lists of frequencies.

"This is getting us into a very difficult spot!" she said in his ear. But for once, she felt he was paying her very little attention.

"This is simply too complicated!" she continued to her friend. "The troops must be dropped by air over the bridgehead in one deployment."

Lordy looked up from his papers, running his fingers through his distinguished grey hair and taking a handkerchief to pat his brow. Nell noted how his perplexed expression had suddenly cleared.

Now he seemed to be listening to her attentively.

"What was that you just said?" he asked her.

Nell didn't need a second invitation and launched into her damning assessment of "Operation Greenfly."

"I was saying that the deployment will not be quick enough if they drop our boys in two sorties!" she explained in a serious whisper. Nell was using every ounce of her ability to make him understand.

"They should use towed–gliders, the ones stationed here, at Tatton!" She didn't stop talking now she had his ear.

"Plus, since we have already bombed the French railways

out of all existence, we can't wait the weeks needed to repair them! It will take thousands of men and prisoners to fix even a few dozen miles!"

Lordy interrupted her at that point. "Now, my dear girl, slow down and start again."

"What do you mean Lordy?" she bent close to him and he whispered in reply; "what was that you said about difficult spots?'"

"It was just that, I said it was a difficult spot. It isn't important."

"Oh yes it is!" Replied Lordy, without checking the volume of his commanding voice.

At this outburst the entire room fell silent.

"Is there something you wish to share, Mrs Layton, or Your Lordship?" spoke the Prime Minister sternly from across the table.

Clouds of cigar and pipe smoke hung low over the huge table. All of the men, nearly all of the most important men in the Western World thought Nell with embarrassment, were now watching her squirm uncomfortably in her chair.

Nell felt flushed as the entire room fixed her with their eyes. She wanted to disappear under the table and be swallowed alive by the rug.

Then she composed herself. She was tired and emotional, but not so worn down that she was going to be dismissed as an impertinent interruption.

She had not sat there for four hours, singlehandedly unpicking these problematic invasion plans, to be made to look a fool by a man of loose morals who only hours ago had been in the storerooms, 'putting his eggs in more than one basket.'

"Apologies Prime Minister." I was just remarking to Lor... His Lordship..." She trailed off as Lordy reached over and took her arm.

"What Mrs Layton means to say is, may she be excused

Sir?" Nell looked at him in surprise. He continued to address the room as he slowly rose to leave his seat. Nell, held tightly in his commanding grip, was forced to stand with him.

"I see no reason why not" replied The Major puffing on his pipe as the room regained its focus. "Neither of you are particularly needed for the moment."

. . .

"What on earth was all that about!" cried Nell as she and Lordy stepped out of the room and onto the veranda.

The air was warm and fresh on her face and she was in a fighting mood.

"And what was that nonsense about 'spots'?" Nell was awash with emotions and the whole day was beginning to catch up with her. She turned now to her companion.

"Please explain yourself."

Nell knew in her heart of hearts that they only had one chance to over-run the Germans dug in along the Rhine.

She knew that the bridges were key and that Operation Greenfly could succeed, but it needed air support, and only with gliders as the main deployment tactic could enough troops land at once and take the German commanders by surprise, and in numbers.

All this had become apparent in the briefing. She had thrown away her one chance to speak and as a lowly Private Secretary this was surely her only opportunity to be heard above the arguments and counterproposals.

And she had blown it.

Or rather, Lordy had blown it.

She looked at him and he lowered his head. Her eyes said everything she could not.

"My dear girl, you are quite right in everything you have said about that buffoon's invasion plans." She immediately felt comforted by his tone.

Fenella Layton was after all a woman of good breeding and intellect and she could recognise when to talk and when to listen.

"Your appraisal of the logistics is correct." At these few words Nell let herself smile.

"However, this is not your most significant contribution to events." Lord Egerton gestured for her to take a walk with him into the grounds.

Nell took his arm and soon the pair found themselves surrounded by the majestic high walls of Tatton Park's topiary hedges. Once he was sure that they were not overlooked, Lordy chose a secluded bench and sat down. Nell followed suit.

"When you spoke back there you said a word to me. It was 'spot!'" Nell looked at him quizzically, although it was far too dark for Lordy to read the expression.

"Do you know what I was looking at, the very moment that you spoke?" He asked.

"No, no I was unsure. Was it radio frequencies or codes?" she replied, completely confused but intrigued as to the direction the clever old man's explanation was taking.

"It was forecasts from the Meteorological Station. The information had baffled us, but I have worked it out, with your help!"

"How so? You must tell me!"

"The data predicts unprecedented sun spot activity in exactly seventy-two hours time. When you used the words 'difficult spot' it jolted my memory." He looked at her and Nell stared blankly back.

"Do you know what a sun spot means?" Nell shook her head.

"All Allied communications will be lost in the solar storm heading towards the atmosphere! Our boys in the second wave will be unable to find their targets, the radio beacons will fail and the paratroopers will overshoot the drop zone!"

"But how do you know such things for sure? You cannot rely on such untested science. This is science fiction!" Nell exclaimed with horror. She stood and began to remonstrate with the noble man.

"I was about to explain to the Prime Minister that gliders we have stationed here are easily able to solve his problems and you have dragged me into the gardens to wax lyrical about the sun!" She was losing her usually calm demeanour.

"Oh, now we are truly lost!" she conceded with a desperate tone in her voice.

"Those over confident Generals and the easily led Prime Minister will surely send our brave boys to their deaths!"

Somewhere overhead towards the walled garden, an owl hooted in the darkness. It seemed to Nell to echo her feelings of loneliness.

Finally, Lordy also stood and moved towards Nell. He joined her where she stood alone on the damp lawn and held her trembling hand.

"My dear Fenella, listen to me." he said softly to her. "We have known each other for many years, I rode and fought alongside your father and your husband, our lives are completely entwined. You and your three beautiful children mean all the world to me. Do you really take me for such as crazy fool that I would let you all down?"

At the thought of her husband, her son and daughters Nell broke down. She fell gently to her knees in the cool grass and wept, Lordy's hand on her shoulder.

After what seemed like hours, but was only a few moments, he lifted her to her feet and kissed her cheek.

"You and I are going to put right all these wrongs, together" she felt his eyes search hers for the spirit he knew burned so brightly inside. Softly he continued and held her close.

Nell could feel his heart beating like a gentle drum, urging her to rally to his flag.

"There was never any chance of those crazed men hearing you out. I had to get us out of there. Tonight, when you are charged with the duty of transmitting the battle plans, you must act, you must change the date!"

Nell was beginning to make sense of it all as he spoke.

"Bring the two troop movements forward, together, in one decisive thrust. Rain the supplies and troops down from the gliders, avoid the solar storm and we will be certain of victory!"

As Lord Egerton spoke, Nell felt herself give way to his will and the starlit sky above her swirled out of control.

CHAPTER EIGHT

Once inside a small private bathroom within the Commandant's private quarters, Mary locked the door from the inside and exhaled for the first time in what felt like minutes. The room was small and rather feminine, lit by a single gold candelabra.

Sure she was safe and alone, Mary finally opened her hand.

The note contained inside was folded four times over; to the size of postage stamp, and when fanned out was no bigger than a postcard. It read:

My English Rose,

If you are reading this it means that the first part of my plan has worked. The moment I heard you were one of the Commandant's dinner guests I knew this could be my only chance. Now I'm afraid you must be brave and ready to help me once more.
I know that it wasn't you that betrayed me before my capture. I know now it was your husband who fetched local goons. I do so hope that there have been no recriminations on you. I don't think I would ever forgive myself if anything ever happened to you my love.
I am determined to escape from this place and am already working on a plan with some of the other chaps in here. I dream every night of escape, only to be with you once more and I promise to do everything within my power to make it happen.
Will you help me now? Come to the east wall of the castle tonight.

Mary did not see Freddie again, but she was strengthened by the knowledge that wherever he was, he would be working on their escape plan.

.

Too–whit too–whooo!

An owl hooted outside of Mary's window.

The sound startled her awake from where she had been quietly dozing in an armchair by the fire.

As she raised her head, the book she had been reading fell heavily to the floor. It made a soft thud as it hit the hearth rug.

Her body started upright and she sat, motionless listening for the smallest sound from any other part of the house. All was quiet.

She bent to retrieve the book, "what was the title again?" She thought drowsily "Oh yes ... 'Open Wings.'"

She realised that she must have barely read the first page before she had dozed off.

She wondered how long she had been asleep. Her neck felt slightly stiff and she was feeling a chill.

Examining the fire she could see that it had reduced to a few glowing embers.

Too–whit too–whooo!

Mary had rarely heard the sound of an owl since setting up home with Heinrich in this part of Saxony.

The sound had always delighted and comforted her.

"Owls are symbols of wisdom" she thought to herself. In ancient Greece, it was believed that they had a magical inner light that gave them night vision, she remembered.

"Are you my protector, little owl?" she whispered aloud.

"Are you my sign of victory? Are you sent to accompany me into the dark foreboding night and to keep me safe?"

THE COLDITZ COCK

Another sound met the delicate shell of her ears.

This time the muffled chimes of the old grandfather clock. It chimed the half hour. It was time to act.

She crossed from her private day room and into her bedroom, grabbed her riding boots and coat and dressed quickly.

In light of recent events, she and Heinrich never shared a marriage bed and with Mary kept herself virtually secluded in her private quarters. Her husband had conveniently gone away on business for the night and would not be present to accidentally catch her on this night-time mission.

Nevertheless, she had no intention of waking the household staff and alerting them to her movements.

Slowly she opened her bedroom door and crept across the landing. Even in the silence of night, small creeks and groans of the old house could be heard.

Luckily, tonight the house seemed to be conspiring with her; the sounds it made masking her careful progress down the backstair.

Once at the side door of the house, it was a short walk to the riding stables, where she had left her favourite horse; Hotspur, saddled up earlier that evening.

She noticed nothing untoward between the house and the stables. A quick glance over her shoulder told her that the house remained completely shrouded by darkness and not a sound could be heard.

Undetected and alone she entered the secluded stable yard.

Hotspur was a handsome, dapple grey stallion and he whinnied as Mary approached, obviously pleased to see her again.

Mary threw her arms around the well muscled neck and inhaled his familiar smell.

She stroked Hotspur's nose whispering to him, "you and I have a mission to complete and I am trusting you with all my heart."

"Calmly and quietly now, Hotspur," she instructed as she led him quickly into the yard. Within moments the pair were away, disappearing under the conspiratorial cloak of night.

"Come on my boy," she urged him as she began galloping across the fields.

Hotspur bent his head low against the wind. Faster they galloped and despite the fear rising gradually inside her, Mary felt free already.

She was an accomplished horsewoman who had been riding all her life and she was comfortable, almost fearless in the saddle. As a younger girl she had dreamt of competing in shows.

Her body swayed to the undulating motion of the horse's flanks as faster and faster they rode, as if chased by unseen demons or a vicious pack of Bavarian wolves.

As they approached the woods at the edge of the estate, Hotspur slowed to take the awkward winding path through the trees.

On the other side of the coppice, Mary knew there was a large but hidden break in the walls encircling the majority of the extensive grounds.

Tonight it would provide an easy exit from her country prison.

This jagged vent framed by piles of bricks was a closely guarded secret held by Gisela and her mother. They used it to go about their private business and to avoid the ever watchful and controlling eye of the master of the house.

Mary had observed Gisela regularly taking the same path into the woods and had one day had resolved to follow her. Unknowingly, Gisela led her to this place and revealed to her a secret way into the outside world.

Why Gisela needed a secret exit was of little concern to Mary now. She imagined it was black market activity or a secret lover. Neither possibility shocked or surprised her.

Mary was purely grateful for the knowledge that she had been unwittingly given.

Now, safely out and on the other side of the wall, Mary urged Hotspur to gallop again.

Across fields they sped, heads down, eyes streaming from the wind. Mary could feel the speed beneath her and rejoiced in their temporary freedom.

"I could keep on galloping like this forever" thought Mary.

Joy entered her heart and she thought of nothing but her and Freddie on Hotspur together as she sped through the night.

Suddenly, out of the darkness before them, the castle was in sight.

Mary's heart skipped a beat as she slowed to a trot and took in the view before her.

Its imposing form loomed out of the countryside and its inner walls appeared to glow from the sinister arc lights that protected every entrance and courtyard.

Tonight it did not intimidate her, for it held the key to her enduring happiness and soon she would have him, have her life, have her enduring freedom.

Approaching the east wall she tethered Hotspur to a post conveniently placed next to a small stream from where he could freely drink.

She whispered quietly in his ear, "now, my faithful one, you must wait here for me. Don't make a sound."

With that she retrieved a lump of sugar from her jacket pocket, placed it in his mouth and stroked his glistening neck.

Turning to the wall of the castle she began scanning the horizon for guards, searchlights or any movement that might betray her.

The castle was still.

Colditz had more recently become notorious for the multitude of escape attempts made by its prisoners, mainly the British.

The guards meticulously and constantly guarded all potential exits, covering all previous escape routes with coil upon coil of barbed wire.

"They were never alerted to the fact that someone might try to break in!" Mary thought to herself. She felt confident that she would not be seen.

She quickly scrambled down the bank into the dry moat and waited at the foot of the wall as she had been instructed.

After five minutes, the moon passed behind a cloud. The searchlights trained on the towers were now the only light. They punctuated the darkness with their brilliance, but left small pockets of black between them.

In one of these pockets, Mary presently saw movement. "Is that him?" she gasped, her legs weakening beneath her.

Then, over the edge of the wall, she began to make out a small flickering white object which slowly drifted towards her.

At first she thought it must be a bird, but as it grew closer to her she realised that it was a plane; a tiny paper aeroplane!

It glided towards her and she reached into the air, stretching with both arms and taking the plane in her hands.

This must be the sign she had been told to expect. She folded the paper and placed it safely inside her bodice, next to her warm skin.

As the moon revealed itself again from behind the cloud, she untethered Hotspur, mounted her faithful steed and sped back to her prison the way she had come.

. . . . .

THE COLDITZ COCK

Alone in the quietness of her own rooms, Mary slowly locked the door. It was dawn and she could finally give herself permission to look at the paper aeroplane.

There were in fact four sheets of thin writing paper and they were crumpled but still intact when she drew them out from beneath her clothes.

She held them to her face and used their worn edges to caress her cheek. Then as the first morning light came through the window and lit the translucent surface, Mary searched out the tiniest trace of scent of the man she loved.

Sitting at her dressing table, she spread out the valuable treasure among the powder puffs, perfumes and lip sticks.

Before her eyes, drawn in fine detail and delicate silverpoint pencil were the plans for a plane, a glider! So, this was his plan; to fly out of Colditz! How ingenious, how daring, how impossible!

"But of course," thought Mary aloud, "tunnelling must be almost impossible now with so many successful attempts having been made."

"The soldiers would never think to look up! Freddie my genius!"

Poring over the tiny writing, Mary quickly familiarised herself with every tiny detail of Freddie's plan.

He seemed to have meticulously calculated the size and weight of each of the minute pieces of the escape glider, to be constructed it appeared, by hand, in scavenged wood and metal.

Every strut and support would be fashioned from stolen floorboards and held firmly in place using handmade nails.

One of the most ingenious ideas of all appeared to be to dope bedsheets with a starchy millet saved from the prisoners' meals.

Mary laughed to herself at Freddie's daring and inventiveness.

But would the plan work? Could the glider fly? His calculations seemed accurate and the drawings he had provided looked convincing.

That morning, Mary did not move from her improvised office. She studied every detail, calculating and recalculating, making endless notes, redrawing sections of the glider again and again.

There was no way that his co-conspirator was going to let Freddie's plan fail. If it took every part of her, this bird would fly him to her safely!

She smiled secretly to herself.

What Freddie could not possibly know, and what now seemed to Mary the most delicious turn of fate, was that she already knew an awful lot about gliders!

Mary's father Gerald Hamilton had been a keen aviator and had spent many hours flying his Tiger Moth bi-plane.

Before his untimely death, caused by the awful wounds he had sustained in the Great War, Gerald had inspired the same passion in his daughter.

They flew together often, and it was Gerald that had taught her everything she knew.

In 1931 they had even entered a Daily Mail competition together, in an attempt to become the first to pilot a glider both ways over the channel.

It wasn't the £1,000 prize that had spurred their interest, but the chance to apply their combined technical knowledge and passion for flying.

They had not won the competition that day, but they had learnt a great deal, and that knowledge was now coming to Mary's aid.

Flying was in her blood and she counted many great aviators amongst her friends; particularly the famous Amelia Earheart.

Amelia had become a family friend on visiting London

after her history-making solo transatlantic flight in 1932.

Mary still had some of the highly fashionable clothes that Amelia had designed and gifted to her.

The flying suit with its loose trousers, zipper top and big pockets had been featured in Vogue. It was a highly controversial fashion range and many society people had criticised the designs in other Society papers for being too masculine.

But Mary had loved the flying suit and even dared to wear it to a party at Tatton. That of course, was before she was married.

Now her dear friend was no more. She had disappeared on that fateful round the world expedition and no trace had ever been found of her, or her plane.

Another tragic loss in the life of such a young woman, it had left a great impression.

But what her dearly missed father and friend had gifted Mary was the knowledge she needed to ensure that rights were wronged and true love would triumph.

In this dark hour, Mary's family and friends would see what she was really made of and they would be proud.

. . . . .

Over the next week, Mary spent each morning in her room working studiously.

She paused only to eat and to maintain the outward appearance of routine.

No one must suspect anything, particularly her husband. Mary had told him that she was preparing her classes for the commandant's wife and he had expressed his approval at her enthusiasm for the task.

Heinrich seemed convinced that he had finally tamed Mary and that she would cause little trouble in the future.

His slackened vigilance had allowed her to slip out and

ride to the castle that night. Now her quiet studiousness was taken for subservience and submission. How little, she thought, he really knew of her!

After a week of arduous study, Mary sat back in her chair, finally satisfied with her work.

It really was a work of art; a full set of plans for a glider that could fly Freddie to freedom.

The original drawings were very good, Mary had known that instinctively at her very first glance. However, she had quickly identified a number of tiny errors which could, if they had gone unnoticed into the final designs, have proven potentially fatal.

"Heaven forbid that Freddie should fall to his death because of my lack of diligence, on such a short flight over the walls and moat – and to me" she thought as she surveyed her work.

In Heinrich's library she had found inspiration too. Tucked away and badly categorised by someone, was a moth–eaten and badly foxed copy of C.H Latimer–Needham's 'Aircraft Design'.

The thick volume did not tell Mary much that she didn't already know, however, its explanations of the necessary physics and engineering were quite instructive. The book also included a detailed diagram of a wing section.

So Mary had painstakingly redrawn the plans from scratch, using the book as a reference, recalculating each number, redrawing each piece of the glider.

She knew that although there would be some basic contraband tools in the prison from tunnelling, the chances that her imprisoned countrymen had successfully acquired the complex and specialist carpentry tools needed for such delicate woodwork, was unlikely.

Mary included in her redraft a complete inventory of equipment they would surely need.

She had even drawn up an ingenious list of everyday objects that Freddie could either find in the camp or procure by blackmailing guards.

These included everything from gramophone springs to window bars, all items that the glider detail could adapt to make saws. There was even Mary's personal favourite – a basic concept drawing for an ingenious set of skeleton keys to be fashioned from a simple bucket handle!

She had thought of everything. Prisoner sleeping bags could be used as glider fabric and a gramophone needle could act as an effective gauge.

Smiling gently to herself, Mary caught her reflection shining back at her from the three angled mirrors of the antique vanity table.

Being so engrossed with her work as an apprentice aeronautical engineer had for a moment eclipsed her more obvious attractive qualities.

The graceful swanlike neck and porcelain skin, her shining eyes, now seemed to radiate intense beauty without the need for mascara or eyeshadow. All fine features that entrapped the desire of every man lucky enough to make her acquaintance.

Mary remembered for a moment how love, beauty and romance had been her guiding lights all through life. Now she felt that valour and honour had joined the list of true feminine virtues

But there was no time to dwell. Mary carefully folded the newly drawn plans and returned them, as she had everyday, to their hiding place under her plain brown dress.

The dress was an old one, once elegant and of the highest fashion. Mary had had the village seamstress alter it very recently, removing acres of ecru lace to render it plain and somewhat shapeless.

It had the dual effect of creating a form which was still

presentable and fitting for a lady of Mary's position, but had plenty of space to conceal the evidence of her and Freddie's secret glider plans.

Also, Mary mused as she stood now before the mirror, the dress had the added effect of completely repelling any unwanted advances from Heinrich.

She patted the dress down and checked the plans were now firmly held. Mary then took the original plans in her hand. Although lothe to do so, she knew that she must dispose of them.

They were her only physical connection to him, paper that had been held in his hand and hers, but she crossed the room and bent down resolutely, placing them in the fire.

Within moments the papers exploded into a blaze of orange and red, then quickly reduced to ash.

Only one small remnant remained intact which Mary carefully moved into the centre of the fire, where it quickly smouldered and disappeared.

"There!" she exclaimed to herself, brushing her hands clean on her drab skirts.

"And now, to my work at the castle!"

CHAPTER NINE

Summer was slowly giving way to autumn across the land.

There was a subtle chill sweeping in from the north and with it came murmurings that German dominance on the battlefield was declining.

Mary sensed that the war was now going quite badly for The Reich.

She had heard that the Wehrmacht was losing ground throughout northern Europe. Rumours abounded in and around Colditz that Hitler had recalled Generalfeldmarschall Gerd von Rundstedt from retirement, a sure sign that things were going badly. He was expected to start reinforcing against an Allied invasion.

On a recent trip to the village seamstress, Mary had witnessed elderly men and boys from the village being rounded up. It had made her cry desperately for hours.

She was not alone in this. On the hill in the prison camp, the inmates of all nationalities were worried. Ripples of terror spread through the barracks. Some were in fear of being accidentally killed by American bombers targeting the garrison at Colditz.

Most were terrified by thoughts of the uncertain fate everyone would suffer at the hands of the Russian bear.

The three beech trees in the grounds on the Von Strauss Estate still stood majestically like large graceful giants, but their once vibrant green coats were slowly fading brown with age.

Their low branches were now welcoming arms to Mary,

who was sitting between them with her eyes closed and her face turned to the weak midday sun.

Mary felt that far too much time had passed since she had first received the escape plans from Freddie and today she would finally have to return to Colditz under the guise of tutor to the Commandant's wife, whose name she'd been told was Elise.

Under normal circumstances, the idea of meeting and conversing with another woman of importance and social standing, above all a woman of class and intellect, would have filled Mary with untold excitement.

Today however, the mild pleasure she felt at widening her social circle was completely engulfed by conflicting waves of dread and excitement.

It was clear in her mind though, that today was the day her plan would be put into action.

Mary had prepared meticulously for this moment and had left little to chance.

Every last tiny detail had been replayed in her head and she was ready.

At two o'clock she would be driven to Colditz Castle by a German officer. She would walk inside and there, if her luck held, she would begin a chain of events from which there was no return.

Mary had not been able to eat or barely breathe all morning. She had been ready, with her bags packed since ten o'clock and now, as she paced around the grounds out of sight of Heinrich and the maid, her heart was beating desperately like a drum inside her. Mary wore a sombre looking grey dress and bonnet, fabric was in very short supply, but the village had provided for her something suitable for the current season. Mary felt that it presented just the right impression of a proper school teacher, without compromising too much the allure of a beautiful figure.

"I must stay calm and focussed," she told herself as she tried to walk off her nerves, "or I will surely be discovered."

"I have already lost my nerve once before and that surely led to Freddie's capture."

The thought of that moment; his face looking at her from the back of the army truck, was enough to cause her to lose her footing and stumble.

Holding onto the trunk of the beech tree to re-establish her balance, she breathed deeply to calm herself. "I... must be... strong, for him," she scolded herself as she returned to the house.

Half past one came and the Commandant's private car drew up to the house. The car was identifiable by its overstretched length, high black lustre and two small flags which fluttered on the fenders, proclaiming the vehicle's occupant's high status within the Nazi Party.

This vision was intended to intimidate and Mary felt it did its job well enough.

Heinrich was waiting on the drive. He exchanged the required salute with the guard and moved forward to exchange a few words.

Mary busied herself collecting her bag and checked in the most casual a way as she could muster that she had absolutely everything that she required.

Ignoring her husband's gaze, she moved towards the car. The guard opened it for her with a flourish, obviously keen to impress Heinrich. Mary stepped inside without a sound.

The guard then offered his leather–gloved hand, gesturing to Mary that he would take her bag.

She instinctively pulled it back towards her body, reacting protectively of its contents. Then quickly correcting herself, she remembered her plan and offered it to the waiting guard with a pleasant smile.

"Thank you", she said in German, "you are very kind."

"It is rather heavy and full of books," she added as she handed it to him.

The guard placed the bag in the trunk and Mary heard the satisfying 'clunk' of German engineering as the boot closed.

The guard returned to the driving seat and started the engine.

"Good–bye my dear," said Heinrich, "I am counting on you to make a good impression." He waved.

"And do not worry. The guard will be with you at all times, to ensure you come to no harm," he spoke without emotion.

Mary was sure that this was a warning rather than a reassurance and she took it as such.

They began to drive away from the house.

As the car disappeared down the drive Mary felt as if she could sense Heinrich's eyes burning into the back of her head.

Although these days he rarely articulated his feelings openly towards his wife, and indeed when he did address her directly he seemed cold but polite, Mary knew that Heinrich harboured a deep resentment and seething hatred towards her.

He carried it inside always, like a concealed dagger, and Mary wondered how long it would be before Heinrich would eventually snap and vengefully lash out at her.

Mary touched the side of her soft cheek as she looked back over her shoulder at her husband, but Heinrich had already turned and re–entered the house.

She felt relief that he, along with the marble column facade of the grand building's portico, were behind her and out of sight. The car turned the corner onto the open road.

· · · · ·

The car travelled in silence for ten minutes, encountering no one on the journey except the usual idle smoking checkpoint guards, who either ignored the Commandant's limousine or waved it through with barely a glance at its lady occupier.

Presently, the imposing facade of Colditz loomed ahead. The whitewashed stone walls gleamed in the autumn light and soon the car was drawing up to the main gate.

The low arch of the entrance was at first glance only guarded by a single armed sentry. Mary felt a chill down her spine as she imagined the hidden soldiers in their gun nests, weapons trained on any and all approaching vehicles, and her!

She tried hard to maintain her composure and looked straight ahead, showing no fear.

The driver and the guard exchanged words with each other. Gestures were made and the guard took a cursory look inside and then waved them through into the dark tunnel that marked the beginning of the prison buildings.

Mary breathed an inaudible sigh of relief as they drove between the deep walls and out again into the light.

As anticipated, the guard had not dared to search Baron Heinrich's wife or ask to check her luggage!

"Besides" she thought to herself, "there is actually nothing of any consequence in there!"

The outer courtyard was bristling with armed soldiers, busy installing new defences and barbed wire.

The car passed by them without stopping and not one of them looked up to notice the beautiful and desirable woman inside.

The suspension of the limousine barely rattled as the vehicle crossed the cobbled bridge straddling the inner moat.

They slowed to a stop and the driver stepped out of the car. Within moments he appeared with her bag, opened Mary's door and she gently placed her feet on the grey stone floors of Colditz. For the time being at least, she was not afraid.

The guard gestured with his hand inviting Mary to precede him and they she began to walk in the direction of the commandanture.

Mary and the guard crossed the courtyard, he with his eyes forward, constantly on her, while all the time Mary tried surreptitiously to scan the buildings for any sight of the prisoners.

It was imperative that evidence of her arrival at the castle be noted by the British prisoners

Mary made sure that her shoes clattered on the stones and alerted everyone above to the fact that there was an elegant Baroness in their midst.

"My love, my love, I am here" the noise of her kitten heels seemed to proclaim.

Making their way to the commandant's quarters on the east side of the main courtyard, Mary stopped abruptly and turned to her escort.

She chose this point in their journey to thank the driver for escorting her so pleasantly; knowing from her previous visit that this is where the British prisoners were kept and would be looking out.

The guard looked confused but smiled politely nonetheless.

"You are most welcome Frau von Strauss." He nodded his head towards the buildings before them.

"This way please."

Mary did not move.

"You have no need to carry my bag, Private," she replied. "I am quite capable and can easily manage," she instructed him with a friendly smile, holding out her lace–gloved hand.

The confused soldier did not question Mary and handed her the bag.

Mary turned and resumed walking, straining from the corner of her eye to see if they were being observed.

As she did so, Mary allowed the bag to drop open slightly. On the very top was revealed a thick blue book.

This was exactly where, on the evening of the dinner, Mary recalled the British prisoners had harangued them.

Now her eyes searched each small window quickly, anxious for any sign of Freddie, of anyone.

It was no use. She could see no one and they were already at the entrance to the Commandant's quarters. Waiting now at the archway for the door to be unlocked, Mary stood with her bag slightly turned towards the windows above. "Please let him see. Let him understand my message," she whispered to herself.

And then the door opened.

"This way please" commanded the guard and she was brusquely but politely ushered inside.

Without another chance to glance behind her she disappeared.

. . . . . .

The Commandant's rooms were in the eighteenth century part of the castle. The walls seemed incredibly thick and didn't retain any of the sun's heat.

The air carried a chill and Mary pulled her coat closely across her.

A long stone corridor led to the library from which a warm yellow light glowed. Mary, carrying her bag, entered silently.

The guard who had escorted her from the door now clicked his heels and saluted the room. He then turned and left.

Mary had at first believed that she had been left alone in the library, which was of average size, windowless and dimly lit only by candles from a central chandelier and the fire in the hearth.

Then she noticed that seated with her back to the door was a woman.

Mary indicated her presence with a tiny cough and approached the table where Elise, the Colditz Commandant's wife, was seated.

Elise stood at once. She was slim, graceful, dark and extremely alluring. She had eyes that slanted up at the corners and a red mouth which curved invitingly.

She was not beautiful in the accepted sense, but Mary realised that she had never before in her life seen a woman's face which was so fascinating.

She was dressed in black with touches of white. Her gown was sophisticated, elegant, Parisienne black and although its design had relieved it of all trimmings, this had only served to increase its stylishness.

Mary had never worn such a gown and had really only ever seen such quality once or twice before and then only in the pages of society magazines. It proclaimed Elise as a woman of sophistication, taste and extreme wealth.

Even now in the dim light of an old library, the choice of such a deep black fabric made her skin appear almost dazzling white and brought out the subtle red highlights in her hair.

Mary shook herself, aware that she must have been staring.

Elise warmly greeted her new visitor in excellent English; "Such harsh times! War is such a man's game, it is such a blessed relief to have some female company." She smiled and held out her hand.

"Welcome to the peace of my little hideout, Frau Von Strauss!" She beamed as she spoke.

Mary stretched out her free hand to greet her, carefully

holding the bag and its books with the other.

"I cannot tell you what a pleasure it was to accept your invitation here. How delightful that we share a love of literature and poetry" Mary said.

As she spoke, she noticed how the warm walls of the library's mahogany shelves seemed to cradle her voice.

"It will be wonderful to read aloud, although you do not seem to require much practice, your diction is impeccable" she continued, "and please, you must call me Mary."

"And you, I insist, must call me Elise."

Mary bent down and placed her bag under a chair, first carefully removing the thick blue book and resting it on the seat. She took off her coat and casually concealed the book underneath.

Mary's outerwear had obscured an elegant outfit; a white silk blouse that lit up her face and a string of pearls that highlighted the delicate hue of her face.

Her green velvet skirt fell in a straight line from her hips. It too had been made in Paris and showed off her slim figure perfectly.

"Please, do be seated," Elise said kindly.

Mary took a chair opposite her host, next to her neatly folded coat.

And so the two women sat, searching for pleasantries to ease the conversation forward.

Mary glanced around her. Three of the walls were lined with shelves of books and she could see from the spines that they were of a similar age to those that Heinrich possessed.

"I see you have many of the classics here," she remarked.

Elise laughed unexpectedly.

"I feel that what you mean to say is that my husband's tastes are rather old fashioned!" The jovial remark needed no response. The Commandant's beautiful wife continued, "I'm afraid I would have to agree. Of course, in these times it is almost impossible to obtain editions of foreign literature, and..." at this point she lowered her voice conspiratorially "...many of my favourite writers in the German language have, how should I put it, been forced out of fashion."

"Perhaps you, Mary," continued Elise, "would like to peruse our shelves and select some volumes which we can refer to in our studies?"

Mary's heart jumped. "Here goes!" she thought, realising that she would have to put her plan into action almost as soon as she had arrived.

"Carpe Diem," Mary thought to herself and she rose from her seat with her book in her hand.

She had reached into the folds of her coat and clutched it between her fingers, and she was sure that Elise had not seen her in the flickering candlelight of the dark library.

As she stood, Mary lowered her hand to her side so that the book could not be seen from Elise's seat at the table.

Slowly she moved to the shelves diagonally opposite, outside of Elise's peripheral vision.

Cautiously, Mary raised the book to eye level where she had observed a space for it on the shelves. Her hand trembled as she placed it on the shelf in front of her.

Nestling there it fitted seamlessly with the other volumes.

"I've done it!" she thought as she stared at the complete works of Tennyson in front of her.

In their one night together, she and Freddie had shared their love, not only for each other, but also for the works of Lord Alfred. And now, this shared literary passion would bring them together once more.

This of course was no ordinary volume!

Mary had spent many hours hollowing out the book to create the perfect hiding place.

Using a small paring knife smuggled out of Gerta's kitchen, she had diligently carved out a hole in the thick book.

She had of course left several pages at the beginning intact and these she had glued down once the contraband was placed inside.

Although it pained her to disrespect great literature and damage a work of art, she had created the perfect smuggling device.

It was a necessary part of her plan and she had completed the task with a glad heart.

Inside that volume, sat anonymously on the Commandant's very own bookshelves, were the complete plans for Freddie's glider!

How daring she had been! "How my mother would be proud of me!" she thought as she quickly chose two other books from another shelf and returned to her seat.

"I think maybe we should read a little Austen and maybe Agatha Christie. A contrasting choice, I trust you will enjoy them both. Let us begin with the Jane Austen..."

Mary opened the volume and the class began.

The afternoon passed quickly for both ladies, Elise revelling in intelligent female company and Mary delighting secretly in the certainty of her ruse.

. . . . . .

> *You pierce my soul.*
> *I am half agony,*
> *Half hope,*
> *Tell me not that I am too late,*
> *That such precious feelings are gone for ever,*
> *I offer myself to you again with a heart,*
> *Even more your own than when you almost broke it,*
> *Eight and a half years ago,*
> *Dare not say that a man forgets sooner than woman,*
> *That his love has an earlier death,*

I have loved none but you,
Unjust I may have been,
weak and resentful I have been,
but never inconstant...

Mary's voice faltered at these words.

It seemed to her as if Jane Austen had written them for her. She put down the book, tears welling in her eyes.

Elise stared at her.

"What is the matter?"

There was curiosity in her eyes too.

"And do not for a minute think that I did not notice that business with the book," she added, pleased with the dramatic effect this revelation would have. For her life was usually far too dull.

"I saw you put it on the shelf at the beginning of the class, in fact I saw you hide it under your coat when you first came in."

Mary gasped in shock. Elise continued, "tell me, what is this about?" Her voice was questioning, not threatening.

Mary turned her sad eyes to Elise. "Please, please help me," Mary pleaded.

"If you cannot, then I will surely fall into the most terrible danger," she shuddered, "I am afraid, very afraid."

"If you do not help me then I shall surely die, if not at the hand of my husband then from a broken heart."

Elise's eyes widened.

"Tell me why you are afraid," she asked. She was looking directly into Mary's eyes and the mixture of passion and fear she found there was hard to ignore.

"Nobody else knows what I am about to tell you, and neither can they find out.

Mary took a deep breath and began to explain; "I have fallen in love. Madly, deeply in love with a man who is a prisoner here."

Elise looked at her curiously as if she was not exactly sure what to make of the story unfolding.

"He is an airman" continued Mary, "a wonderful brave, handsome man and I love him like I have never loved before. We met shortly before he was captured and bought here. In that book, there is a letter to him, a love letter, which he will retrieve shortly after I have left."

Mary turned to look at the book, still placed on the shelf. "Please, if you understand anything about love, then let him find that letter."

Yet again, Mary had told a half truth as the whole, complex story was too difficult to explain.

Besides, she did not know how far Elise could be trusted and the best way to gain her cooperation was surely to appeal to her understanding of the affairs of the heart.

Elise took Mary's hand in hers, "does Heinrich know how you feel?" she asked somewhat naively.

"Certainly not and please promise me, on everything you hold sacred that you will not tell him." Mary took a shuddering breath.

"I love him as I have never loved anyone else." Mary's voice faltered.

"This must be awful for you. And you must be desperate to risk your own safety in this way. It really is an act of madness, or perhaps," Elise's voice trailed off.

Mary could bear it no longer. Turning away from Elise, Mary's shoulders shuddered with vast sobs.

"The world is such a complicated place. But this is not complicated, it is simple. You love him," whispered Elise. "Yes, yes I do!" exclaimed Mary.

A surge of compassion and warmth came Elise.

Mary let her body relax and cried all the thousands of tears she had hidden from the world for so long. "I am a woman," she sobbed, "and I need to be loved, to feel love."

"I understand," Elise replied softly. "If only you realised how your words touch my heart. I too feel love and passion." She spoke softly. "But I lack the courage you have shown and I have put away thoughts of love and tenderness in exchange for safety and security."

Composing herself sufficiently to speak, Mary spoke, "Thank you, oh thank you. You are a true friend. I will never forget this, never." She took Elise's hand and kissed it gratefully.

As if suddenly resolving to compose herself, Elsie withdrew her hand and stood. "I must leave now," she said. "We will say no more about this. I promise to speak of it to no one as I am sure you will too."

Elsie walked towards the door; "Follow your heart Mary. You are lucky to have found a true love who returns this love in equal measures to you. But be careful. Heinrich is a ruthless man. He will not let you go."

And with that, she was gone.

CHAPTER TEN

Somewhere a cock crowed.

In the distant rooms of the house, Nell was aware of the sound of plates being cleaned and the clatter of porcelain and silverware from the kitchens.

She opened one eye.

The telegraph machine on the desk near to where her head rested, must have been churning out its paper all through the night and into the early hours of the morning.

Light was beginning to shine between the curtains of her improvised office.

Nell realised that she must have briefly dozed off.

"Oh my goodness!" she said to herself and sat bolt upright in her chair.

Nell was wearing a full length white nightgown under a simple tartan dressing gown.

She reached up to her head and realised that her hair was definitely not looking its best.

There was no one around and she was alone. "I wonder what happened?" she thought. "And where is Lordy?"

As she grappled to steady her mind, Nell reflected on the events of last night as they gradually returned to her.

Suddenly her concentration was interrupted by the telegraph machine. She reached over and tore off the last sheet of paper it had ejected and read.

".....Message confirmation....please repeat Go code.... Message confirmation....please repeat Go code..."

Before she could decide quite how to respond, the figure

of the Prime Minister's wife appeared at the door.

"Knock Knock!" she said, pretending to tap on the open door, "may I come in, I have something I need to thank you for."

Charlie entered the room. Nell noticed immediately that her face was dramatically different from yesterday, and suddenly, as her memories from the previous night returned in a rush, she recalled why.

"This was exactly what the doctor ordered!" Charlie spoke gesturing towards the pink negligee she was wearing. Nell couldn't help but notice how it revealed every detail of every curve of the Prime Minister's wife's glamorous figure.

For a moment she wished that she had not carried out her carefully contrived cupid's mission, and kept her bow and arrows for herself.

"I can't believe you brought this for me! Oh, and the perfume!" gushed the re–born Charlie, "such a wonderful idea! 'The Right Honourable Gentleman' really got a treat!"

She approached Nell and kissed her on both cheeks, holding her face in her hands as she did.

"I think I can safely say, Fenella, that you have saved my marriage and probably the country. John and Charlie Charleston are back and very much in love! I've never seen him so happy!"

Nell was pleased, if a little shocked that she barely remembered coming back into the house and secretly placing the night gown and perfume in the Prime Minister's wife's bathroom.

It had of course been her plan all along, the incident with the maid and her employer had only served to galvanise her spirit and resolve.

However, how this delicate operation had actually been achieved now seemed unimportant. Especially now that Nell could see the dramatic effects. "True love, she thought to herself, will indeed conquer all hearts, eventually."

Just at that moment, the telegraph machine once again clattered into life and Nell remembered with a start, that her work was not yet complete.

Charlie noticed too the machine's insistent 'tap,tap,tap' as it typed another message and she made towards the door.

"I will leave you to your work my dear! I'm going back to bed," Charlie chuckled to herself and Nell could not help but smile, happy for them both. "I don't expect we shall be seeing the Major until long after breakfast has been served!" she remarked, half jokingly, after Charlie as she skipped merrily away along the landing.

Nell now alone again, turned her attention back to the job in hand.

".....Message confirmation....please repeat Go code.... Message confirmation....please repeat Go code..."

Nell now remembered the code name she had given to her and Lordy's plan and entered it with speed and efficiency using the Morse Code device connected to the telegraph cable. Moments later there came the reply

"......Message received and understood.....green for Go.... green for Go....message ends."

Her job done, Nell retired to bed even though the sun was clearly rising on a fine and sunny day.

Before many hours had passed, she would be awoken again by the steady drone of friendly aircraft departing from the Ringway, with their precious towed cargos behind them, heading for the Rhineland.

CHAPTER ELEVEN

The long German winter had come and gone; the numbing cold and huge log fires replaced by warm air fresh with the scent of flowers.

The grounds wore all the gaiety of the new season. Buds were bursting on the trees and tulips had begun to push their way through the earth.

Heinrich and Mary were making their way, side by side, across the lawns. Mary kept a slight distance from her husband.

Their scheduled afternoon stroll was taken by mutual agreement in silence, but so as to follow protocol, together.

If Heinrich was to be found at home at three o'clock, he expected his wife to join him for a walk, without argument.

Heinrich whistled for his two handsome gun dogs busy rooting out a rabbit from under a nearby bush; they did as he bade them, immediately.

He bent down and rewarded them by roughly stroking their heads.

He ran his fingers through his own tousled hair and stood proudly, surveying the scene around him.

Heinrich spoke the first words either of them had exchanged in what seemed to Mary to be hours "I suggest we go back and take tea," he said as he turned and without pausing to see if she obediently followed, headed back to the house.

Mary followed behind him somewhat automatically, her mind totally occupied with thoughts elsewhere.

She hastened her steps as they reached the house.

Heinrich walked towards the Drawing Room, whilst Mary made a mumbled excuse, and turned directly to the stairs that led directly to her private rooms.

She couldn't bear to be in the company of her husband a moment longer than was necessary and took any opportunity to avoid being alone with him.

As she ascended the stairs, Mary thought to herself how Heinrich had become more and more irritable of late. This, Mary attributed both to Germany's fading fortunes in the war, the dreadful winter they had endured and of course the mounting hostility at home.

Heinrich's irritability also had a tendency to turn to anger and both herself and the house staff bore the marks of this.

Heinrich was now physically repulsive to Mary and she could barely stop herself from flinching when he came near her.

Mary had felt the final remnants, the remembrances of love, slip away once he had betrayed her trust and informed the local Nazi militia of Freddie's presence on the Estate.

The cruelty he had dealt to him that day, witnessed by Mary secretly from afar, had shocked her to the core.

She saw Heinrich for what he must always have been; a brutish man hungry for power and influence, without an iota of real courage.

She was and probably always had been his prize, his trinket, to be played with as he saw fit.

Or so he thought.

. . . . .

Over the long winter months, Mary had continued to communicate with Freddie through a series of night time escapes to the castle.

Just as she had done on that first visit, Mary sped through

the night, carried by her faithful Hotspur to the walls of the castle.

There she would wait for Freddie's messages to gently sail down to her through the air.

The first time she had returned, Mary had sat for hours staring up at the walls, waiting for evidence that her love had been alerted to her English lessons with the Commandant's wife and gained access to the Library.

She had read the letter as soon as it had floated into her hand, there on the banks of dry moat in the cold autumn moonlight.

My dearest Mary,

How wondrous it was to see your face as you walked through the prison yard. I am sure if you could even see me at the high window!
How I yearned to touch you, to hold you and to kiss your precious lips. You really are a wonderfully clever woman; I knew immediately when you looked up, that the book was meant for me.
Of course, I could not see the title, but I was sure that there would be some clue or other to help me.
I had to wait a full twenty four hours to gain access to the library. The guards these days are easily bribed, luckily one could be convinced to let me borrow some books, and he only looked briefly when they were returned, to make sure I hadn't torn out the pages to use as writing paper!
It took me a couple of minutes to find the book, but when I did; Tennyson! Of course. How could I forget the wonderful night we spent together talking, laughing, how quickly I fell in love!
Even more miraculous than the wonderful plans you sent back to me is the knowledge that you feel the same way I do.
And those plans! I really do not know what I would have done without you.
Conditions here are not always the best and some days, food is scarce. It's pretty difficult to concentrate what with the constant roll calls and all

the confusion caused by the almost constant escape attempts.
The other night, one of our men; a brigadier made it out. We're hoping for a home run, as so far he's not been caught.
He hid in a rubbish cart, no idea how he managed to fold himself up so small, but he got away with it!
The poor blighter had to hide in a stinking pile of rubbish for an age, but when the coast was clear he changed into a Nazi uniform and just walked out of the main gate!
I have the plans and your note explaining your routine of visits to the castle. I wait for your next ingenious parcel.

All my love
Yours, forever
Freddie

Every week Mary hollowed out a new book of poetry, and every week, she returned to the castle to tutor Elise. No further mention had been made of Mary's imprisoned love and Mary knew, as she arrived before Elise and left after her, that she made no attempt to retrieve the supposed love letters or to read them.

Mary banked on the obvious affection Elise felt for her and her compassionate understanding of the importance of love.

She was as sure as she could be that Elise would not betray her.

. . . . . .

Freddie had worked tirelessly on the glider with a group of British comrades at Colditz.

He had obeyed Mary's new plans exactly, trusting her superior skills and judgement implicitly.

An excellent workshop had been set up behind a false wall

in the attic above the castle's unused chapel and the men worked painstakingly, long into the night.

The rollcalls kept everyone on their toes and it took a large number of prisoner stooges to keep lookout.

From the first call of 'appell' until the complete courtyard roll call was taken there was just five minutes to stop work, conceal the evidence of the workshop and make it down to the yard.

On many occasions Freddie and his men nearly didn't make it in time.

He and the men were understandably proud of their efforts.

Each of the hundreds of wooden struts was shaped by hand from a bed slat. Then the wing struts were individually fashioned from levered–up floor boards.

"How on earth did they manage to get away with that?" Mary sometimes thought to herself.

Most of the materials were scavenged, a few obtained through bribery and the rest; smaller items, smuggled in by Mary on her weekly visits to the library.

She had been asked to sneak in ingredients for glue, nails and even bits for a drill, all of which had taken a few weeks to bring inside in small batches.

Mary had managed to procure all the requested items from the abandoned barn and workshops on the estate with little difficulty.

The only dilemma had been how to conceal them from Heinrich and the staff.

In the end she had decided on a loose floorboard which easily lifted and was concealed under a small Axminster rug.

And now, as their labours were nearing completion, one final communication from Freddie had been retrieved;

CARTLAND INSTITUTE FOR ROMANCE RESEARCH

My darling

In haste. We are ready. The runway on the roof is nearing completion.
It has been decided that I will make this escape on my own.
The glider has more chance of making a good crossing over the river with only one passenger on board.

Expect news within a few days.
Allied Forces are approaching fast.
Jerries here are getting nervous.

If you hear of imminent danger, come immediately to the castle as planned.

Soon we will be together.
Forever yours,
Freddie

CHAPTER TWELVE

"Destroy... evacuate!?"

"Are you sure?"

Heinrich's agitated voice could be heard booming through the house.

Mary raised her head from the book she was half–reading in the drawing room and listened intently. The situation was clearly deteriorating quicker by the hour.

"Yes, yes, of course. Immediately. I will release the staff and make my own preparations." Heinrich put down the telephone receiver and strode purposefully into the drawing room.

He stood with his legs apart, hands on hips, fixing Mary with a purposeful stare.

"Colditz has received orders to evacuate. That means the Allies are close at hand. You must make immediate preparations for our departure. We leave in the morning."

Without expecting or waiting for a reply, Heinrich turned to leave.

"But are we not safer here?" Mary feigned alarm, but secretly a mood of intense anticipation was building inside her.

"Safer perhaps...for you. But we are leaving together, husband and wife. Do not question me. If we get caught I will need you with me, to provide me with safe passage." He was of course right, Mary knew this and had expected the day to arrive when suddenly her husband would take a renewed interest in her value to him.

"Anyway, you should think this through properly dear,

if we stay, there is no guarantee that the allies won't shoot first and ask questions later. And then we'll both be done f..." Heinrich's words were suddenly eclipsed

Boom! Boom! Boom!

The first sound of the approaching Allied field guns shocked both of them. They were indeed closer than the pair had imagined.

Despite the obvious fear etched deep into her face, Mary did not seek solace in Heinrich's arms.

Instead she sat very still, listening to every shot, every explosion, trying to estimate how far away the troops and the moment for her to act might be.

Mary knew that the order "destroy evacuate" meant that the German army were preparing to evacuate Colditz and possibly take at least some of the prisoners with them as hostages.

British Officers in particular could be very useful as bargaining tools and to ensure the fleeing Nazis' safe passage.

"Freddie will surely be shipped out under the cover of darkness with the others" thought Mary. "We must go to-night!"

"I will pack a few small bags, I presume that is acceptable to you?" she enquired after her husband. "Yes, but only what you can carry," replied Heinrich. "I will release the house staff to fend for themselves."

Mary turned away from Heinrich so that he would not see the hatred spread across her face. As she turned, he marched from the room.

"Gerta and Gisela!" inside she cried inside desperately and thought to herself; "They have served his family loyally their whole lives and now he tosses them aside like worn boots. How I loathe him."

Mary knew that she would have no time to bid farewell to her faithful servants and that she would probably never see them again.

"At least their papers will identify them as civilian staff in her employment and they will most likely be left alone by the Allied forces." Mary tried to comfort herself with these thoughts.

Then quickly the focus of her attention shifted.

Mary realised that Heinrich would even now be distracted, readying himself for their escape the next morning and that she must go to Freddie right away.

"If I do not go now" she thought, "Freddie may be marched away or even shot. Even if we did both get out of this alive, we might not see each other for years."

The thought of this turned her stomach. Her mind raced.

"And besides, I am not as safe with Heinrich as he seems to think he is with me. I have no idea what he might do if he is cornered, and I am not going to stay to find out!"

This was now becoming a very real fear for Mary. She had seen the growing desperation on his face and the evidence of his recent physical outbursts with Mary and the staff was enough to make her mind up.

"Heinrich, I will be ready in two hours," Mary said.

He hardly heard her.

His mind was full of his escape plans and how he might use his English wife to his best advantage.

Unknown to his wife, elsewhere in the house, Heinrich was even now weighing up his options.

At that moment he was considering surrendering directly to the British and in this way, he thought he could avoid the risk of internment altogether.

Mary alone in her bedroom changed her clothes.

She still had that famous Earheart flying suit and she found herself hastily stepping into it, then zipping it closed.

On top of the flying suit, she put on a pair of pleated trousers, a loose, long sleeved blouse and a square shouldered jacket, all in carefully selected drab colours.

She looked slightly dishevelled as the material of the trousers kept awkwardly catching on the flying suit, but from a distance, her appearance was relatively normal.

"For once, no one will be paying any attention to what I am wearing anyway," she said aloud and smiled nervously to herself.

A small suitcase was already packed and hidden under the bed.

Inside were some personal toiletries, a nightgown, gloves, undergarments and a change of clothes.

Into this case Mary carefully placed photographs of her family, her favourite brooch and a small selection of books. "Just the essentials" she told herself.

There was no time for sentimentality.

Mary quickly looked around the room to ensure that she had left no clue as to her escape route.

There must be nothing for Heinrich to find.

She knew that before long he would no doubt angrily tear the room apart. How her husband would rage!

As ready now than she felt she would ever be, Mary quietly checked that the hallway was empty and then closed the door of her room behind her.

Heinrich could be heard giving final orders to the staff and his stern voice rose through the house from kitchen.

Mary seized the moment and crept ever–so carefully downstairs and slipped unchallenged into the Drawing Room.

The large window by her favourite chaise was still open, just as she had left it earlier that day.

For the past week, Mary had taken to planning her escape on an almost hourly basis and always had at least two convenient ways out of the house prepared.

An agile woman and with little fear these days, Mary easily clambered out of the window and pulled the suitcase easily after her.

She walked stealthily over the gravel until her feat touched the soft velvet cushion of grass and then broke into a silent run.

Running faster than she had ever done in her life, she headed for the safety of the old barn.

Gasping for breath she reached the door and pulled on its huge weight, levering with her whole body, until it was fully open.

She hurried to what would appear to a casual eye to be a pile of straw and began frantically throwing huge handfuls and whole bails aside, panting as she lifted each one.

She stopped momentarily only when her breath left her completely.

Her chest heaving, she lifted bale after bale and slowly, a large, black shape emerged; a small black van

Once she had completely uncovered the secret escape vehicle, she threw her case onto the back seat, felt for the key in the ignition and started the engine.

It purred into life.

"First time!" Mary exclaimed as she looked through the small windscreen and assessed her way forward.

"Oh no!" She exclaimed quietly.

Out of the barn doors, Heinrich could be seen in the near distance, striding purposefully across the lawns towards the trees and the barnyard.

He was holding something in his hand and Mary knew instantly what it was; a hand gun.

"Would you really shoot your own wife?" Mary shouted, although he was still to far away to hear.

She put her precious escape vehicle into gear and pressed her foot firmly on the accelerator.

As she raced through the barn doors, taking part of it clean off the hinges, she could see Heinrich's furious face trying to take aim at the van.

"Goodbye Heinrich. You cannot control me!" She shouted through the window.

"You never really did. Now it is your turn to fend for yourself."

The black van sped away in a cloud of dust, along the gravel path, past the lake, the house and out of the main gates.

Heinrich lowered the gun and stood frozen, watching in disbelief.

CHAPTER THIRTEEN

Driving fast along the country road as dusk fell, Mary was still gasping for breath.

Her heart pounded in her chest and she anxiously turned to look behind her every few moments, from fear of being hunted.

She felt the wonder of her escape sweep over her and this calmed her breathing.

Mary's foot was pressed hard on the accelerator.

She took each corner at great speed and without the aid of the van's headlights; spinning the wheel to avoid skidding into the surrounding fields as they appeared in the gathering darkness.

The sound of shelling could be heard from all sides over the roar of the engine and the sky on the horizon was alight with explosions.

"It must be the Americans" thought Mary.

As she rounded another bend, Mary was forced to swerve to avoid the burning wreck of an armoured personnel carrier. Flames lit up the whole lane and Mary had to shield her eyes.

Her wheels screeched as she flew past, keeping her head forward and her eyes focused on the road, for fear of seeing the poor soldiers whose own escape had obviously not succeeded.

The horizon opened as she drove on and into the darkened fields either side of the road Mary was aware of the occasional hunched and running forms of German infantry, fleeing in the opposite direction to her.

Now in her peripheral vision, Mary could clearly see the flashes of small arms fire. The smell of burning and cordite was everywhere.

As she rolled at speed around one final bend, Colditz Castle loomed into view.

The searchlights that she had avoided on her night time visits to the castle were mostly shot out, only one or two still scanning the sky, frantically.

As she approached, the walls of the fortress were lit mainly by shells exploding overhead. Occasionally, a well-targeted shell from the still distant artillery hit the castle squarely with a shocking thud and Mary winced as she thought of Freddie. Part of the Commondanture near the British barracks was clearly ablaze.

Again flashes of machine gunfire exploded from the hills behind the castle.

"The German army is fighting back hard!"

"What do they think they are still fighting for?" she asked herself.

Suddenly a shell screamed above. Mary instinctively swerved, as an explosion some way in front of her shot up a wall of earth and tarmac; the sound of the blast following only after the debris had begun to fall to ground. A huge smoking crater remained.

The shock of the blast eventually reached the side of the still moving van and Mary gasped for breath, struggling to control the vehicle.

Another whistle told of a second shell exploding overhead.

This time she slammed her foot down hard and the car spun a full three hundred and sixty degrees before coming to a stop.

Desperately turning the key and pumping the accelerator, Mary frantic with terror and the urgency of her mission willed the car to start again.

She looked to the sky, searching for help from God, from the stars, from anyone or anything.

"Freddie!" she shouted frantically, her hands still clasping the wheel, her anguished voice directed at the stars above.

As if answering her cries, the silhouetted form of their elegant glider appeared before her on the horizon. It swooped low directly towards her, along the line of the damaged road, sailing in and out of the billowing curtains of dust left by the exploding shells.

"Freddie!" she cried again, this time with relief. "Freddie!"

Out of the van Mary leapt, arms waiving a white scarf above her head. She was not sure if he could see her or the van.

Freddie was no amateur pilot and even on this, the glider's one and only flight, he controlled it with supreme skill and precision.

Mary felt the wind from the glider swish through her hair as it passed so close overhead that she had to crouch down beside the van.

"Is he playing with me?" she thought.

Behind her she distinctly heard the loud thud of the glider's skids hitting the road.

Thud, thud, thud! The glider bounced to a stop, spinning slightly around as its left wing tipped to meet the ground.

Following the trajectory with her eyes, in the gloom she made out a cloud of dust where Freddie had landed.

Shells continued to fall in the surrounding fields and Mary ducked instinctively with each deadly thud. The arcing explosions all around the glider strobed and illuminated the tight fabric of the tail fin.

After a few seconds a shadow emerged from the cockpit.

Freddie was walking towards her calmly, with a flying helmet under his arm!

As he caught sight of Mary standing there, he could not help but break into a run.

Mary matched his stride and in the middle of the deserted road they fell into each other's arms.

"You can put those kites anywhere!" he laughed as he gazed into her eyes.

"I thought you were going to land on the roof of the van!" she replied.

He drew her close in the kiss that they had been yearning for.

It was a kiss of trust and joy and a promise of all the years to come.

They tightened their grip on each other and his lips were on hers, with a passionate tenderness.

Mary felt at one with him, they were enveloped together in such a powerful, passionate embrace that neither of them could have any doubt about their feelings.

For a moment it was impossible to think, only feel. Not only did his whole body become part of her, but his heart and soul were as well. They belonged to each other.

Their lips parted for a second and they stood mesmerised by the intensity of their romance. Shells and guns blazed in the air all around them, but neither of them flinched or even seemed to notice.

Finally Freddie spoke, "I love you, Mary...with all my heart."

"I shall make sure that we shall never be parted again."

"And I love you, my darling, darling Freddie."

He tilted his face up to hers and kissed her again, tenderly and slowly at first and then with a deep passion.

They were soaring, flying together in the ecstasy of love and of a new life to come.

EPILOGUE

Somewhere unseen among the trees, birds were calling to each other.

On the majestic lawns of Tatton Park a blackbird hopped along cheerily, its beak full of fluffy nesting materials, plucked from the borders.

Maurice Egerton stood on the veranda, surveying the bucolic scene, leaning on the stone balustrade and smiling broadly to himself.

From behind the mansion a formation of spitfires could be heard returning from another successful sortie.

"So you are back with the land of the living?" he said without turning around.

"Feeling refreshed?"

"Yes, thank you for asking." Nell stood with a brimming mug of hot cocoa and she approached the nobleman, stepping out through the elegant opening of the French windows. It was past noon.

"Congratulations are in order, don't you know?" He spoke warmly.

Even though she couldn't see his face, Nell knew instinctively that her accomplice was grinning with satisfaction. Lordy continued.

"Word has come back that the daring early morning mission was a complete success."

"Apparently," he paused, "it owes its success entirely to it having been brought forward and carried out in one single massive raid."

"The Germans don't know what hit them. Intelligence reports say that all the major targets have been achieved and Jerry is in full retreat!" Triumphantly he turned to face her. "It's all your doing, Nell."

"Well now, I can't take the credit for everything!"

"Actually, rumour this morning around the PM's staff is that you can!" He paused and stroked his chin. "Who would have thought that the Prime Minister's Private Secretary would find the time to not only save his reputation as a great wartime leader, but also to save his marriage!"

Nell's jaw dropped with shocked surprise. But there was no time to deny anything.

"Speak of the Devil!" Lordy nodded his head in the direction of the mansion.

Nell turned around and there in the door was the Prime Minister, still in his pyjamas, filling the pipe in his hand.

"I think I'll make myself busy elsewhere," said Lordy to Nell and he began to trot off briskly, in the general direction of the Walled Garden.

Then he stopped and about–turned, scurrying quickly back, as if he had forgotten something important.

"You didn't eat any devilled eggs yesterday, did you Nell?" Lordy asked quickly.

"No, why ever do you ask?" exclaimed Nell, surprised at the question.

"I only ask because both Nigel Stalker and his insufferable wife have been carted away in an ambulance, salmonella poisoning apparently. Dreadful affair!"

He winked and before she could respond was off across the veranda, in the opposite direction to the approaching Prime Minister.

"Good morning Nell!" called the Major across the veranda "What a truly wonderful day!"

Nell, her guard down, took a little risk.

"Good–afternoon!" she corrected him. There was a notable pause.

"Yes, yes, quite so." He seemed relaxed, when normally such a response would have annoyed him terribly, thought Nell.

Also she noted to herself, he seemed not at all embarrassed to be stood dishevelled and blinking in the early afternoon sun, still sporting pyjamas, dressing gown and slippers.

He flapped comically over to her in his unsuitable footwear.

"I have a bone to pick with you, private secretary." He addressed her pointedly, but Nell thought there was also a hint of humour in his tone.

"Yes, sir?" Nell had no idea what was coming next.

"A little bird told me that somehow, between you receiving my orders last night and them being transmitted to the Field Commander, a little confusion might have occurred..."

His question tailed off and he peered closely at Nell, looking quizzically at her over the top of his glasses.

She thought that he was searching for signs of some further insubordination, or evidence of guilt. In fact he was toying with her.

"Not only did someone change the plans dramatically and all for the better it seems, but I might add, they changed the name of the whole mission!"

"Now I have my suspicions that Lord Egerton is behind the change of plan," the Major was grinning slightly as he spoke "but 'Operation Back to Basics' has you written all over it!"

About the Authors

The Cartland Institute for Romance Research (CIFRR) exists to explore the life and work of the celebrity romance novelist, political activist and aviator Dame Barbara Cartland. Established for Tatton Park Biennial in 2012 by Ultimate Holding Company, CIFRR is located in a purpose built mobile research station, created by the artists.

Ultimate Holding Company (UHC) is a group of creative pioneers and provocateurs operating at the junction of contemporary visual art, engaged design practice and social activism.

The organisation is concerned with the process of collective production, social solidarity and the role of artists and designers in creating sustainable communities.

To this end UHC locates its practice in collaboration and co-authorship, making work that is characterised by no one specific media or material, but that stands apart through the craftsmanship, warmth and intelligence of its aesthetic.

@UHCstudio | Tweet about this book using #CIFRR | www.uhc.org.uk